An unforgettable Hollywood princess in a small
southern town, Divine Matthews-Hardison is the star of
Jacquelin Thomas's popular series

Simply Divine   Divine Conf...
Divine Mat...

"There's something compelling about Divine and her amusing take
on life."   —*Booklist*

"Funny, heartwarming, spiritually uplifting. . . . A page-turning story
that's sure to touch lives."

—ReShonda Tate Billingsley, bestselling
author of the Good Girlz series

"Down to earth and heavenly minded all at the same time. . . . It
made me laugh and tear up."

—Nicole C. Mullen, Grammy-nominated
and Dove Award–winning vocalist

"A good dose of fashionista fun."   —*Publishers Weekly*

MORE ACCLAIM FOR THE WONDERFUL FAITH-BASED
FICTION OF JACQUELIN THOMAS

"Touching and refreshing."   —*Publishers Weekly*

"Bravo! . . . Sizzles with the glamour of the entertainment industry
and real people who struggle to find that precious balance between
their drive for success and God's plan for their lives."

—Victoria Christopher Murray, bestselling
author of the Divas series

"A fast-paced, engrossing love story . . . [with] Christian principles."
—*School Library Journal*

Split Ends is also available as an eBook

More Divine Books by Jacquelin Thomas

It's a Curl Thing
Divine Match-Up
Divine Secrets
Divine Confidential
Simply Divine

Split Ends

Jacquelin Thomas

G

GALLERY BOOKS

New York   London   Toronto   Sydney

Gallery Books
A Division of Simon & Schuster, Inc.
1230 Avenue of the Americas
New York, NY 10020

First Gallery Books trade paperback edition March 2010

GALLERY and colophon are registered trademarks of Simon & Schuster, Inc.

For information about special discounts for bulk purchases, please contact Simon & Schuster Special Sales at 1-866-506-1949 or business@simonandschuster.com.

The Simon & Schuster Speakers Bureau can bring authors to your live event. For more information or to book an event contact the Simon & Schuster Speakers Bureau at 1-866-248-3049 or visit our website at www.simonspeakers.com.

Illustration from istockphoto.com

Manufactured in the United States of America

10 9 8 7 6 5 4 3 2 1

Library of Congress Cataloging-in-Publication Data

Thomas, Jacquelin.
    Split ends / Jacquelin Thomas.—1st Gallery Books trade pbk. ed.
        p.   cm.—(Divine and Friends series)
    Summary: Preferring homelessness to living with her irresponsible mother, teenaged Kylie runs away, takes a job at a hair salon, and learns to trust God.
    [1. Interpersonal relations—Fiction. 2. Beauty shops—Fiction. 3. Homeless persons—Fiction. 4. Runaways—Fiction. 5. African Americans—Fiction. 6. Christian life—Fiction. 7. Pacific Palisades (Los Angeles, Calif.)—Fiction.]
    I. Title.
    PZ7.T366932Sp 2009
    [Fic]—dc22
                                                                                    2009006314

ISBN 978-1-4165-9879-4
ISBN 978-1-4391-1583-1 (ebook)

To my children—
I'm so blessed to have you in my life
and it's an honor to be your mom.

Acknowledgments

To my readers—thank you so much for the never ending support and your love for Divine and friends.

Split Ends

Chapter 1

My worst nightmare has come true.

Here I am, living on the streets, walking around looking all dirty and smelling like a polecat on moonshine as my grandma would say. Being homeless is one thing, but having to walk around stinky is just the worst thing ever.

A week ago, I left the apartment I lived in with my mama. We were about to be evicted unless she could talk or sleep her way into another apartment. I hate thinking about my mom in this way, but truth is truth—that is what my Grandma Ellen used to say.

To be honest, I miss my grandmother. We lived with her in Statesville, North Carolina, before my mama decided to up and move to Los Angeles after a man. This same man dumped her before we were even in town a whole day.

Instead of going back home with our faces cracked, Mama decides that we're gonna stay out here. She's got this big idea that she can star in a music video or become an actress. All I can say is that it's fixing to come up a bad cloud.

My mama's real pretty and she knows it. She's young, only fourteen years older than I am, but since I didn't ask to be here, she should at least try and act like a mom. I cannot stand her irresponsible ways, the way she dresses, parties, and steals. She needs to grow up and start acting like a normal parent.

If Grandma Ellen hadn't died six months ago, I would've gone back to North Carolina, but now I have nowhere else to go.

Well, I could go back to the apartment, but I'm tired of living like that—having to move in the middle of the night because she'd rather look fly than pay the rent. It is so embarrassing to have to tell my teachers that the reason I couldn't finish my homework or study for a test is that we didn't have lights. That instead of paying the bill, my mama would go shopping.

Just two weeks ago, I had to go down to the jail with her because she was caught shoplifting some skimpy lingerie.

She got mad at me because I wouldn't let her pass that stuff to me. I am not a thief, so I left the store and waited for her outside. Just as she strolled out as if she owned the place, we got hauled back into the store by an undercover detective. I just wanted to die right there on the spot.

It was a blessing that Mama didn't have to spend the night in jail. One of her old boyfriends came and paid her bail. I had to place several calls before one would even agree to help us.

I couldn't take no more of the drama, so that's why I ran away. If Mama ends up in jail, then I would have to go to foster care, and if we get evicted, which I'm sure we will, I'll be where I am now.

Homeless.

A dirty braid falls across my cheek as I lower my face on the approach of a passerby. I don't like looking into their faces and seeing the varying looks of pity or disgust.

I glance across the street at the hair salon watching the woman who I assume is the owner take a carton of supplies out of her car. I heard that she lets the homeless come in and wash up from time to time before the salon opens or in the evenings after it closes.

Not many people like me come by much—mostly because of where the shop's located, and the fact that she has a police officer hanging around in the evenings.

Even from where I stand across the street, I can tell this isn't your regular, everyday beauty shop. It's fancy and, from the cars that the clients drive, very expensive.

Yesterday, I ventured closer to steal a peek inside. There were six stations with black granite countertops, and huge mirrors covered red walls. All of the hairdressers wore black with red aprons and their hairstyles on point.

I got here early this morning in hopes of seeing if she would let me come in to get a good shower and maybe get my hair washed and conditioned.

The thought makes me wrinkle my nose. I can't deny that I could use some deodorant. I haven't had a bath in a week. The June heat is hotter than a frying pan popping grease all over the place. Soon I won't be able to stand myself.

I swallow my pride and hold my breath as I rummage through the crumpled, grease-stained fast-food wrappers, coffee cups, and unrecognizable stuff, looking for cans in the trash area situated behind the restaurant located across from the Crowning Glory Hair Salon.

I back away from the trash, gasping for a whiff of fresh air. I fight the urge to throw up by reminding myself that I need enough cans to recycle and get bus fare. When I'm done, I'm going to find the nearest public bathroom to wash my hands.

I glance over my shoulder in time to see a girl around my age walk out of the Crowning Glory salon. She stops just outside the shop and watches me for a moment.

I am so embarrassed right now that I wish the ground would open up and swallow me. She's already seen me picking through the trash, so there is no point in running off. Instead, I pretend that I'm not aware she's staring me down. I hope that she'll have the good sense to just move on, but she doesn't. She walks to the end of the sidewalk as if waiting for the traffic light to change.

When it does, she comes across the street.

I look down at my stained T-shirt and torn blue jeans, a contrast to her starched and pressed denim, her eye-popping pink shirt and matching bangles. She has her chin-length hair pulled back in a ponytail.

My stomach does a nervous flip when I realize that she is coming in my direction. A wave of apprehension washes over me and for an instant, I consider taking off running. For some reason, though, I can't make my feet move.

I sure hope that she is not a whack job or anything. She might be the type who can't stand homeless people. I'm feeling lower than a snake in snowshoes. The last thing I need is a beat-down from a complete stranger. She might think I've been trying to case the shop or something.

I look up, meeting her gaze. I know one thing. If she comes here trying to get in my face, I'll get with her, no problem.

She looks uncomfortable so I speak first. "Hey."

"Hey," she responds, eyeing me from head to toe. "I'm Rhyann. I saw you hanging around the shop yesterday and

I want to give you this," she states, holding out five or six dollar bills and a five.

I hate the look of pity I see in her eyes. I survey her nice jeans and silk shirt. Her sandals are fierce. I don't even own a pair other than my four-dollar flip-flops. When I left home, I only took what I could fit in my backpack. Right now, she is eyeing my raggedy Converse sneakers.

"I know that it's not much, but it'll get you something to eat," she tells me.

I smile and she smiles back.

"Thank you," I say, taking the money out of her hand. "I appreciate it. Oh, my name is Kylie."

"Do you have somewhere to stay?" Rhyann asks me.

I nod. "If I leave now, I can get a bed at the mission."

I can tell she doesn't like the sound of that. "Stay safe," she replies. "I hear it can get pretty bad out there."

"Thank you, Rhyann." I point across the street. "You work there?"

"Yeah, I do."

"Your boss—she'll wash my hair?" I ask. "I heard that she lets people like me come to the shop to get cleaned up."

Rhyann nods. "Miss Marilee is a really nice person. She'll wash your hair for free. Why don't you come to the shop with me right now?"

I hadn't expected to do it right now. I summon up the courage to walk across the street with her so that I can ask about getting my braids washed and do a lil' bit of cleaning up, but just as I make it to the curb, a Mercedes pulls up and parks. A woman gets out and walks into the shop.

I'm not about to go strutting in there looking and smelling like I do with one of her clients present, so I tell Rhyann, "I'll come back another day. Maybe tomorrow morning."

She looks at me. "You're sure?"

"Uh-huh. She's got a shop full of clients, and I don't want to go in there like this," I say quietly.

She sees that I'm embarrassed. "Okay, but I'm going to let Miss Marilee know to expect you, Kylie."

"I'd appreciate that. Thanks Rhyann."

"Hopefully, I'll see you tomorrow. I'm not working until eleven o'clock."

I watch Rhyann until she enters the shop. I can't believe how nice she's been to me. Deep down, I look forward to seeing her again. I hope that maybe we could become friends. I haven't really made any since we arrived in California, mostly because we moved around so much.

My stomach growls, reminding me that I haven't had anything to eat since the cheese and crackers I ate last night.

"Get a job," a man mutters as he brushes by me.

His words sting my already rock-bottom ego.

"I would if I could," I whisper. "It's not like I want to be out here, but I'm only sixteen."

People like him don't really see me—they just see someone who lives on the streets. I am a teenager just like any other teen. I worry about stuff like school, peer pressure, and boys, so I'm not so different.

The only difference between me and other teens is that I am no longer in school and I don't have a place to live. I never stayed in the same one the entire school year because of moving from place to place. I always feel like I am missing or leaving something behind because of all of the moving I have had to do.

At least I have enough money for bus fare. I'll take the bus downtown to Fifth Street, where the Safe Harbor Mission is located in the heart of skid row. I heard some other homeless teens talking about it last night.

I hated sleeping in that abandoned building, even though it was a group of us together. I met them my first night away from home, and when they invited me to hang with them, I agreed because I was too afraid to sleep on the streets alone.

Some of them left this morning to try to steal some food. That is not what I am into so I decided not to go with them. One of the girls has a drug problem and she is thinking about prostituting her body to make money. I definitely don't want to do that, so I said my good-byes and headed off in a different direction.

I break into a sprint down the sidewalk. It's hotter than a two-dollar pistol, as Grandma Ellen used to say. And I'm sweating bullets.

The first bus that comes, I say to the driver, "I need to get to the Safe Harbor Mission. Is this the right bus?"

He nods sourly.

I give him the money, then walk all the way to the back and sit down, hanging my head low. I hope I don't offend anyone with my smell. The stench from the trash mingled with my perspiration is a stinky combination.

During the ride, I try to wrap my head around the idea of Rhyann being so nice to me. She doesn't know me or anything, but she still gave me ten dollars. I haven't met many people like her. Then my thoughts drift. I pray that I'll be able to get into Safe Harbor or one of the other shelters. I don't want to have to stay on the streets another night. I heard about this homeless man who was burned alive.

My chest tightens at the thought. I close my eyes and count slowly, waiting for the terrified moment to pass.

I don't know what's going on with me, but sometimes I feel like my breath is getting cut off. I think it comes from being scared and stressed out from worrying about my mama and the crazy stuff she does.

The driver lets me know that I should get off at the next stop.

"Thank you," I say before stepping off the bus.

One of the teens told me that the Safe Harbor Mission had a program called Safe Sleep and I am hoping I can get in. I didn't feel all that comfortable with those kids. Their desperation and willingness to break the law reminds me of my mother and how I ended up in my current situation.

This man wearing a purple suit gets out of a Lincoln

Town Car and walks up to me, grabbing me by the arm. "C'mere, pretty girl . . . I got something for you."

"You don't have nothing I want," I reply, trying to pull away. "Leave me alone," I shout, hoping someone will help me.

"Look, I'm just trying to help you out. I can get you all cleaned up. Buy you some clothes and make you feel good."

"I don't need your help," I insist. "Let go of my arm."

He gives me a hard stare. "You being mighty ungrateful," he tells me. "I'm trying to do you a favor."

A woman pushing a shopping cart across the street stops walking. "Let her go!"

He cusses at her.

She pulls a bat out of the cart. "I said, let her go, before I come jerk a knot in your tail."

From a distance, she looks like a fragile old woman wearing camouflage pants and a black T-shirt, but the way she is swinging that bat, it's clear that she knows how to use it.

"This is my woman," he argues. "We're just having a little spat. Now go on and mind your business."

"I don't know you," I say loudly, my heart racing. My chest starts to hurt, and it is getting hard for me to breathe. "L-let me g-go."

"If you don't let that child go, I will crown you with this bat," the woman warns as she crosses the street. "You think I don't know what you been doing? You won't snatch another girl to prostitute for you if I can help it."

"Shut up, old woman," he snaps, his grip tightening on my arm.

She speeds up her pace. "You get them hooked on drugs. I know what you been doing. You don't scare me. I'll whup you like a rented mule. Now let that child go." The woman positions herself with the bat held up, as if she's ready to play baseball.

A tense few seconds pass before he growls, "You ain't even worth all this trouble." He suddenly releases my arm, then shoves me hard toward the woman.

She catches me before I fall. "You all right, honey?"

I nod. Up close, the woman doesn't look as old as I initially thought—she's probably in her mid- to late forties. With all that gray hair, I thought she was around sixty years old.

She moves around me swinging her bat. "If I ever see you near this girl again I'll kill you. Do you hear me?"

"I don't want the skank," he mutters. "I couldn't even give her away for free." He walks backward to his car.

"One day you'll come looking for Lucky D."

"I doubt that," the woman shoots back. "Ain't nothing you can do for her. Just get in that overdecorated heap of junk you call a car and get on from here."

He lets loose another string of profanity.

The woman just laughs, which seems to make him angrier. In warning, she holds up her bat like she's about to take a swing. "I said git on out of here."

He jumps into his car and hightails it out of there, tires screeching in protest.

She watches him go. "Praise the Lord that I was able to get to you in time. Lucky D is a pimp, and all the time he trying to pick up girls, looking to fill his stable. He don't care how he get them. It can be snatching them off the street and getting them hooked on drugs."

She surveys me from head to toe. "Let's get you inside the mission."

I try to calm my nervous stomach and my trembling body. "Do you stay there?"

"Yeah," she replies, parking her shopping cart against the building and grabbing her shopping bag. "When I can get a bed. Sometimes I stay outside in the courtyard when they run out of beds, because it's much safer than the streets."

"What if that man comes back?"

"Then I'll have to kill him dead," she says, matter-of-fact.

"I mean that," she tells me when I gasp in surprise. "Lucky D looks for girls that are all alone in the world like you. Are you out here by yourself?"

I nod.

"Well, you ain't alone anymore." She grabs the door and holds it open for me. "My name is Lucy."

I smile. "I'm Kylie." When we're inside the lobby of the mission, I continue. "It's real nice to meet you, Miss Lucy."

She smiles back, despite the fact that she looks like something is hurting her. "I can tell by your accent that you're a Southern girl like me. Where do you hail from?"

"Statesville, North Carolina."

"I'm from Georgia."

"We almost moved to Atlanta once," I say. "But then my mama met this new guy and liked him better than the one in Georgia so we came here instead."

"Where is your mama now?" She walks toward a window with a sign that reads FOOD VOUCHERS.

"She's out here," I respond, following her.

Miss Lucy stops and turns to look at me intently. "Honey, did you run away from home?"

"Yes, ma'am," I answer, keeping my voice low. "But it wasn't because I didn't like my mama's rules or anything. I left home because she don't want to be a responsible parent. We're about to get kicked out of our apartment because she doesn't like to pay bills. She is always looking for some man with money to take care of us. I got tired of living off a strange man's wallet."

"I'm sorry to hear that," Miss Lucy says.

"If my grandma was still alive, I could go back to North Carolina, but she died back in December. I don't really have any other family. Not that I'm close to, anyway."

The woman behind the glass smiles and greets us with a real friendly tone. She gives me and Miss Lucy each a voucher for food.

"Thank you," I say, glancing around the room, noting the photos of people, framed and hanging on pale green walls. Poverty-stricken men and women litter the medium-sized lobby area, some talking to volunteers and others sleeping or watching television.

"This is the way to the dining hall," Miss Lucy directs. "What about school?" she asks as we walk down the long corridor.

"I missed most of the last semester," I respond. "But I'm hoping to go back in the fall."

She catches me eyeing her hair. "In my family, we turn gray early," she explains. "I've been like this since I was in my twenties." She goes through her shopping bag and pulls out a shirt. "I think this will fit you. I don't have any pants that will fit you but you might be able to find some inside the mission."

"Do you think they'll let me take a shower real quick? I don't want to go another minute without clean-smelling skin."

Miss Lucy gives me an understanding nod.

Just then my stomach growls, announcing another need I have.

"I know the feeling," Miss Lucy says with a chuckle. "I was just heading back for lunch. They give you three hots."

"I'm starving," I confess. "All I had to eat last night was some cheese and crackers."

Miss Lucy speaks to one of the volunteers who, in turn, escorts me to the bathroom and finds a clean pair of pants for me.

When she leaves, I remove my clothes and turn on the shower. The hot water feels good on my skin. I rinse out the dirt from my braids as best I can. A couple of my braids come out along with my hair, a reminder that I really need to get them taken out.

I dry off with a fluffy towel and get dressed in the clean clothes. I pull my braids up into a ponytail with a rubber band.

"Don't you look cuter than a teddy bear," Miss Lucy tells me when I stroll out of the bathroom.

"That shower really gave me a clearer view of the world," I say, repeating something I'd heard Grandma Ellen say.

We get in line for food.

My mouth waters at the sight of tender-looking meat loaf, mashed potatoes, green beans, yeast rolls. We have a slice of lemon pound cake for dessert.

Miss Lucy and I find two empty seats and sit down to enjoy our lunch.

"This is five-star dining to me," I say. "Mama and I eat mostly fast food or TV dinners. She's not much on cooking unless she's trying to impress one of her boyfriends."

"I pray she comes to her senses before it's too late."

"Me, too."

After lunch, I stop by the library to select a book to read. I spot the latest issue of *People* magazine and grab that, too.

Miss Lucy and I settle down in the TV area along with some of the other women. While they watch some movie on Lifetime, I scan through *People*. I pause to read the article on Kara Matthews and Kevin Nash. Their engagement and upcoming wedding is the talk of every gossip magazine. There is a photo of Kara with her daughter, Divine.

Divine has the perfect life.

I can tell from the photos that she and her mother are very close. It's the type of relationship I wish that I had with my mother. I bet Divine tells Kara everything. My mama and I barely talk, and when we do, it's about some stupid man.

Glancing around the women's dormitory in the mission, I release a soft sigh. The reality is that I'll never meet someone like Divine.

Chapter 2

After breakfast the next morning, I tell Miss Lucy that I am going back to the beauty shop to get my hair straight. I'm tired of walking around here with hair that looks like it's been on the losing end of a catfight.

"You be careful now," she says. "Kylie, make sure you are aware of what's going on all around you. Other people might be paying attention when you ain't, honey."

"Yes, ma'am," I say. "I'll be right back as soon as I can, Miss Lucy."

"I'll be looking for you, Kylie," she tells me. "But before you go, let's have a word of prayer."

We bow our heads and hold hands while Miss Lucy prays for God to keep watch over me. I leave the mission with Miss Lucy walking me to the bus stop, just in case Lucky D is lurking around somewhere. She says that a man like him doesn't always give up that easily when he wants something.

The bus arrives ten minutes later.

I spend my time on the bus thinking about my mom. As much as I hate to admit it, I really miss her. I consider going to the apartment after my appointment with Miss Marilee to see if my mom's still there. Maybe we can talk and work things out.

Half an hour later, I arrive at the beauty shop. I walk inside, looking for Rhyann. Then I remember that she's not scheduled until later. I hope that she spoke to Miss Marilee about me coming.

A woman wearing a red apron over a black shirt and pants comes over to where I'm standing. She gives me a quick once-over with her eyes. "Good morning. I'm Miss Marilee Pittman. What's your name?"

"I'm Kylie."

Her sharp eyes survey my face. "Do you have a last name, Kylie?"

"Yes ma'am," I respond. "It's Sanderson. My name is Kylie Sanderson."

"Kylie, you must be the young lady tha[...] about. I'm glad you decided to come back."

"Yes ma'am, I am," I respond. "Miss Mari[...] like to get my hair washed real good. I've taken ou[...] of my braids as I could . . ."

She nods in understanding. "Have a seat, dear," she s[...] then starts to inspect my hair. "How long have you ha[...] your braids in?"

"Going on twelve weeks now," I respond. "I usually keep them in for about six weeks and then take them out."

"We'll get the rest of them out, and then I'll shampoo you with Surge Power Wash Shampoo and condition you with Infusium 23. I'm really concerned about your edges."

I gaze at Miss Marilee's reflection in the mirror. "Are you sure you want to go to all this trouble? If you just want to wash my hair for now, I'll take the rest of the braids out later."

She shook her head. "Hon, you came to me to help you with your hair, and that's what I'm going to do. I'm not about to have it said that Marilee Pittman allowed your hair to fall out."

I break into a grin. "Thank you."

I work the braids out in the front while Miss Marilee removes them from the back of my head.

"Your shop is really pretty," I say. "It looks high-class. Miss Marilee, I really appreciate your doing this for me, because I'm sure I can't afford to use the bathroom in here otherwise."

to think that my services
"
rject. "Look at all you're

of us—to be kind and

t and my hair is look-

"Now, dear," Miss Marilee says to me. "I'm going to ... your hair and apply a deep conditioner. You won't be able to get a perm for another two weeks unless you want to grow it out natural."

"Do you have to cut off a lot of it?"

Miss Marilee shakes her head. "I don't think we have to trim any more than an inch. Once we get all of the damaged hair off, your hair will grow back in no time."

"Can you cut it into a bob?"

"Yes, I can do that. It'll come just below your ears."

That's an idea I've wanted to try out for a long time. "I think I'll look okay with that hairstyle. I don't want to be walking around looking crazy."

Miss Marilee chuckles. "I'm pretty sure you won't have to worry about that."

She shampoos my hair, slaps on conditioner, places a plastic cap on my head, and sends me to sit under a dryer.

"Would you like a bagel or something?" she asks.

"Thank you, but I've already eaten," I respond, but then

reconsider. I don't know when I'll get my next meal. "Actually, if you don't mind . . . I will take you up on your offer. I have a long bus ride back downtown."

"In that case, I'll make you a bagel with cream cheese and some fruit. How about that?"

I can't believe how nice she is. "Thank you."

Fifteen minutes later, the dryer stops just as I finish off the last of my bagel. Miss Marilee takes the paper plate from me and guides me back to the shampoo bowl. She rinses out the conditioner and says, "Take a seat at my station."

I do as I'm told.

She uses a brush and a blow-dryer to dry my hair. I check out a fashion magazine as Miss Marilee works her magic on me. She's doing such a nice job on my hair, but the reality is that I won't be able to keep it up if things don't work out with my mom and I end up going back to the mission.

As if she can read my mind, Miss Marilee says, "If you have a scarf, just wrap your hair at night. It should come out fine."

"I do have a scarf," I reply.

That seems to remind her of something. "Kylie, I have some clothes in that bag that should probably fit you. They're yours if you want them."

My eyes meet hers in the mirror. "I don't want charity, Miss Marilee. To be honest with you, I really need a job," I say. "I don't know if you need any more help but I could sweep the floor and clean up the bathrooms around here. I don't mind hard work." Seeing that she's even considering it, I add, "I really need a job—any job so that I can find a place to stay."

"What about your parents?"

"My parents are dead," I state, instantly regretting the lie as soon as the words leave my mouth. I can't take them back, though. "I just recently lost my mama."

In a way, it was true, I reason. I keep losing her to those no-good men she's always chasing after.

She replies thoughtfully. "I *can* use someone to answer the telephone and schedule appointments for me. Part of your duties will include working the shampoo bowl from time to time. I'll show you how to wash hair."

I grin. "Miss Marilee, you seem way too good to be true. I really appreciate this so much."

"I'm the lucky one," she responds. "Now I don't have to worry about hiring someone. I can take that off my To Do list."

"I'd like for you to take a portion of my first check for these clothes, please," I say. "I feel better when I earn my keep, if you know what I mean."

Miss Marilee smiles at me. "I believe I do. Why don't you go over to the bathroom and take off those clothes so that I can wash them? I'll have them clean for you when you start work tomorrow."

"Thank you."

I walk out a few minutes later wearing a pretty jade green

shirt and a pair of jeans that are a size too big for me, but since the shirt is long it doesn't look too bad.

"You look very pretty," Miss Marilee tells me.

She gives me a tour of the shop.

One of the hairstylists arrives, and Miss Marilee introduces China as her daughter and co-owner of the salon. "Kylie is our new receptionist."

"It's nice to meet you," China says with an easy smile. "I'm looking forward to working with you."

"You, too," I reply.

"Do you want to fill out your paperwork now, or would you rather wait until tomorrow morning?"

"I can do it now."

"Your hair looks cute," China tells me. "That cut really looks nice on you."

"Your mama hooked me up."

I follow Miss Marilee back to her office to fill out an application, W-4 form, and another form stating that I am a legal resident of the United States.

I have a job!

I thank Miss Marilee for about the hundredth time before walking out of the shop with my hair looking fierce and wearing clothes that aren't stained with dirt and perspiration.

It's interesting to see how people respond to me looking this way. Before the hairstyle and clean clothes, I was treated like dirt.

While I wait for my bus to arrive, I sit down on the bench, humming softly. Two other buses come before the downtown bus rolls in. I quickly get on and make my way to the back.

I sit with my eyes glued to the window, staring at the palm trees and brightly colored exotic flowers and plants dotted all around Los Angeles. It's a beautiful city, just like Mama said, but I still miss Statesville and Grandma Ellen.

I take the bus to Berber Court where I used to live with my mama. At least, that was the last place we lived. If she didn't come up with any rent money, then she got evicted.

I get off on the corner and walk past the park.

My steps speed up, because I need to know if Mama still lives in the apartment. The thought of never seeing her again makes my heart race. After a brisk two-block walk, I glance up at the sign advertising a month's free rent in faded letters stretched across the front of the apartment building. I breathe a sigh of relief when I see our car, a dusty black 1990 Ford Explorer parked out front.

Just then my mama gets out of the car, laughing and talking on a cell phone. Some thick, thug-looking dude gets off, puts his arms around her, and plants a kiss on her cheek.

She is so wrapped up in him and gabbing on the phone that she does not see me standing there. I stare at their backs until they enter the building.

I knew this was a big mistake, I think as I turn and head back in the direction of the bus stop.

Mama does not look like she's missing me at all. It's like

she's glad I'm gone. I can't deny the hurt I feel all the way to my soul. How can she choose a man over her own daughter like that? I love my mama—I really do. I just don't think she loves me as much in return.

My eyes fill with tears and overflow, streaming down my face as I walk down to the park located in the next block.

There is no way I can go back home. My mama is never going to change, and I can't keep living this way. I give in to my anger by wishing that God gave me another mother—one that knew how to act like a normal mom. I really do love her but I also don't like her a lot of times.

I sit in the swing for a few minutes to rein in my emotions. I'm not so sure how I feel about that. Mama works my last nerve and all, but I don't want her to disappear from my life.

Leaving the park, I spot a public phone and navigate toward it, biting my bottom lip.

What if the number has been disconnected? How do I find my mama?

I breathe a sigh of relief when I hear the ringing on the other end instead of a recording.

"Hello."

I'm shocked when my mama answers.

"Hello, who is this?" she asks. "Kylie, is this you?"

I don't say anything.

"Kylie, honey, just say something, please," she begs. "I know it's you. Look, everything is fine. Clyde paid the rent for us so that we can stay in the apartment. Of course, he's moving in but it's only to help us out. You can come on back home. We don't have to move."

I sigh in frustration. Why would I want to go back there with some thug living in the apartment?

"It's just temporary," Mama quickly interjects. "Kylie, why won't you talk to me? Tell me where you are? Honey say something . . ."

"I just called to see if you were okay," I inform her. "And to let you know that I'm okay. I don't want you to worry about me."

Not that you were.

"You need to come home, Kylie."

"Mama, who is Clyde?"

"He's my man."

"What happened to Jake?" I question. "I haven't been gone that long. When did you meet Clyde?"

"Kylie, c'mon, don't give me a hard time. I really like this guy." She pauses for a moment, then says, "Come home so that you can meet him. I just know we're gonna be one big happy family."

"I don't think so," I say. "But I'm glad you weren't evicted. Mama, I need to get off this phone."

"Kylie . . ."

"Bye Mama."

"Tell me where you've been living. I want to know how to reach you."

I hang up the phone, fighting back tears.

When I finally make my way to the bus stop, the one going downtown arrives within minutes, which pleases me because I can't wait to get back to Miss Lucy.

I probably would have gone back home if Mama hadn't been with that thug; the man was uglier than a lard bucket of armpits. Grandma Ellen said that a few times about the men Mama brought home from time to time.

During the bus ride, I think back to the good times I used to have with Grandma Ellen. Hot tears spring up in my eyes once more.

I miss her so much, and I believe she died because we left her all alone. She and my mom didn't always see eye to eye but Grandma Ellen loved her. She loved us and we left her. We never knew that she had cancer. When she finally told us, everything kinda happened real fast.

Grandma Ellen was gone.

Now I'm all alone.

A couple of girls get on the bus at the next stop. They talk and laugh, oblivious to everyone around them. I bet they have been friends a long time. I miss my old friends back home in North Carolina. I haven't really made any out here yet, except for Miss Lucy. It would be nice to find some friends my age, too.

"I wasn't expecting you back here. I thought you'd be able to work things out with your mama," Miss Lucy tells me when I get off the bus.

"Some things never change," I respond, taking a seat

beside her on the bench. "My mama's mind is on a man, so there's no room for me. That's the way it's always been with her."

"I'm sho' sorry to hear that."

"Me, too," I say in a whisper. I hate being out on the streets, but right now it's better than being home with my mom and all her drama.

"I'll keep your mama in my prayers."

"Thank you, Miss Lucy. She needs all the prayers she can get."

"I guess we best be getting down to the mission." Miss Lucy rises to her feet. "We don't want to miss out on a bed tonight."

I stand up, too, saying, "I sho' don't. I'm not crazy about sleeping on the streets." I was so scared that night I spent with those other kids in that abandoned building. I couldn't sleep good because I kept hearing people walking by, talking, cussing, and even fighting over drugs.

We stand in line to see whether we will end up sleeping indoors or in the courtyard of the mission. I'm hoping for a cot inside, but if we have to sleep in one of the tents out back, I'm okay with it. At least we'll be safe.

After we are assigned beds for the night, Miss Lucy and I head to the cafeteria to get something to eat.

I pick up a tray, hand it to Miss Lucy, then grab one for myself. "I want to learn how to make collard greens, too. I love them."

"Have you ever had mixed greens?" Miss Lucy asks. "I make mine with collards and mustards."

"No ma'am," I reply. "But I'd like to try it."

After dinner, we leave the mission to go search for cans. While we walk, Miss Lucy tells me a little bit about her past. It turns out she was in the army. She describes what it was like for her during the Gulf War.

"I'll never forget the morning of March tenth in 1991," Miss Lucy says. "We were positioned near the banks of the Euphrates River when two trucks raced through our position at roughly four in the morning. We opened fire. One truck was carrying fuel, and it splashed its burning cargo on the other. Burning men ran everywhere, only to be met by our machine gun fire. This was my first tour." She shakes her head. "Those images have never left me."

"Why did you decide to join the army?"

"I was bored with working in an insurance broker's office," Miss Lucy replies. "I just couldn't handle the mundane day-to-day tasks of an office job and I didn't want to settle down. I married young and he wasn't a good husband—I never had any desire to get another one. Anyway, I joined the military because I could travel and see the world and have an interesting job."

"Did you still feel that way after you went to the Persian Gulf?"

She nods. "I did two tours over there. Despite the horrors

I've seen, I enjoyed my job and would probably still be in there had I not been diagnosed with scoliosis."

Miss Lucy points down at her camouflage pants. "I wore this uniform proudly."

She stops at an empty lot and says, "Let's look over here. The more cans we find, the more money we'll get."

"How much money can you make selling cans?" I ask.

"We get five cents a can," she responds. "But we can make up to a dollar on some bottles."

"Is that why you have the shopping cart?"

Miss Lucy nods. "I need something to carry them in. I get tired quick and can't always carry stuff in my arms or even my backpack so I put them in here," she says, pointing to the cart.

"I heard a lady say that she was gonna sell blood to make some money."

"Yeah," Miss Lucy says. "You can make between twenty-five and thirty dollars giving blood to the blood bank."

I frown. "I don't like needles."

"I'm anemic, so I can't give any," she tells me. "I need to keep what little bit I have."

I am totally against having someone stab me in the arm with a needle, but since we need money, I may have to get over my fear. "Can I give blood?"

"You have to be at least seventeen years old."

"Oh." Relieved, a grin creeps over my face. "When I get through this," I say, "I'm gonna come back and help out here at the mission. I'm gonna volunteer. I didn't really think much about the homeless people I used to see, but now that I'm in this position, I'm gonna do whatever the Lord leads me to do."

Miss Lucy waves away that idea. "Kylie, you can't save the world, so don't go thinking that you can," she advises. "Some people out here don't want to be helped. You're right about letting the good Lord be your guide, though."

We don't speak for a while after that. Finally, I ask her a question that's on my mind. "Did your mama love you, Miss Lucy?"

Her answer takes me by surprise. "She loved me just like your mama loves you, Kylie."

I fold my arms across my chest. "If she loves me, then why is it that she forgets all about me whenever a man looks her way?"

"Kylie, I don't know your mother, but I'm sure she loves you. I guess she's probably lonely and looking for love, or maybe she's trying to create her impression of the perfect family—you know, mommy, daddy, and children."

"Those men don't want to marry her," I say. "There's only one thing they want from my mama."

She knows what I mean. "You're very angry with her."

I don't deny it.

"Miss Lucy, I have every right to be upset with Mama," I tell her. "I wouldn't be out here living on the streets if it wasn't for her."

"Honey, it was your choice to run away," Miss Lucy feels the need to tell me.

"I felt like I had to leave. I didn't like the way some of those men were looking at me. One of her so-called boyfriends even tried to step to me, Miss Lucy. If my mama loved me so much, then she shouldn't put me in danger."

"Did you tell her what happened?"

I shake my head. "I'm not sure she'd believe me. Serena Sanderson only thinks about herself."

She can see how angry I am. "You know, life out here ain't easy, Kylie."

I try to lighten up. I touch her arm. "That's why God sent me you, Miss Lucy. I know that it's not by accident that we met. Grandma Ellen used to say that there are no accidents when it comes to God. There's only purpose."

"Your grandma was a smart woman."

I smile and nod. "She was the smartest woman I know. I miss her so much, Miss Lucy. I miss my mama, too."

"I just believe in my spirit that the day will come when you and your mother is gonna be reunited. I really believe that."

I sigh in resignation. "I wish I had your kind of faith, Miss Lucy."

"So what do you plan to do?"

"I plan to stay here with you, Miss Lucy," I respond. "I read about teens getting emancipated so that they can live on their own. I'm going to do that as soon as I can afford it."

"You're going to need an attorney for something like that," Miss Lucy warns me.

"I'm aware of that."

"Well, if we're going to stay together, we need to see if we can get family housing in one of the shelters. I don't know if they'll let us without you being my child."

That sounds like a great idea, and I grab on to it with both hands. "They won't have to know, Miss Lucy," I tell her. "It's not like we have to show a birth certificate. Besides, it will only be for a little while. We will stay there until we get our own apartment."

Her patient eyes study me. "I guess it won't hurt us to try."

I break out in a big grin. "I can't wait to get a place of our own. It doesn't have to be a huge apartment—just room enough for the two of us. That's all we need. Then I can go back to school and finish up."

"I sho' hope that you have college in your future," Miss Lucy comments. "I see the way that you read whatever you can get your hands on. You love books and you love to learn—Kylie, you have to go to college."

I'm not so sure about that idea. "I want to, Miss Lucy, but that will depend on my financial situation at that time. I know that I can probably get student loans. I'll spend the rest of my life paying them back if I have to," I say to her.

"They have grants and scholarships available, too. What were your grades like?"

"I'm an A student," I tell her proudly. "My GPA was 4.0 but then we moved here and I missed more days than I attended, with moving around and everything." That's another reason I'm mad. "I don't know what it is now—I missed some of my midterms and a couple of finals."

"I have no doubt in my mind that you'll be able to catch up in no time. There are some online classes for high school students. We'll go down to the library one day and research them."

"Sounds good to me," I respond. "I want more than anything to be able to graduate on time if at all possible. The sooner I get to college, the sooner I can get that piece of paper and change my whole life around."

Chapter 3

I slip on a red-and-white-striped shirt and a pair of black jeans. My flip-flops are red, so I wear them instead of my ratty Converse shoes. I want to look nice for my first day on the job, but this is all that I have. Besides, Miss Marilee understands my situation.

I'm too excited to eat breakfast.

"Honey, you need to put something on your stomach," Miss Lucy tells me. "Take you some fruit to snack on."

"I'll get some fruit to take with me, but right now my stomach is too nervous for me to eat, Miss Lucy."

I glance over my shoulder where people are in line for cold cereal and say, "I might take a box of that cereal, too."

"You have enough money for the bus fare?" Miss Lucy asks. "You got enough to make it back downtown?"

"Yes ma'am," I say. It feels good to have somebody really care about me.

Although I know Miss Lucy isn't feeling her best, she walks me to the bus stop. She's worried that Lucky D might come back around looking for me.

"I'll be here waiting on you when you get off work," she says.

"Miss Lucy, I want you to try and take it easy," I respond. "I know that you're not feeling well."

"I'll be fine."

"I mean it," I say to her. "Get some rest. I know you're in pain, Miss Lucy. You don't have to meet me. I know to be careful."

"I'll be right here. Lucky D's been sniffing around the mission again. I'm not gonna take a chance on your life."

The bus arrives.

I give Miss Lucy a hug before saying, "I'll see you later."

She waits for the bus to take off before making her way back to the mission. I hope she takes my advice and takes it easy. I'm really worried about her.

When Miss Marilee arrives, I am waiting patiently outside

the shop. My bus dropped me off a block away at fifteen minutes to nine.

"Good morning, Kylie."

"Morning," I respond with a smile.

"How long have you been here?"

"About fifteen minutes. I wanted to make sure I wasn't late, especially on my first day."

"That's an admirable quality in an employee. We're all very glad you're here, Kylie, so just make yourself comfortable."

Miss Marilee holds the door open for me.

I follow her inside, where she disables the alarm.

"I picked up a couple of black T-shirts for you," Miss Marilee tells me. "I see that you already have some black pants. I bought you a pair just in case and some black ballet shoes. I bought a size seven and an eight because I wasn't sure of your shoe size."

"I wear a seven," I say.

"Then I'll keep the eights," she decides aloud. "Mine are worn down almost to nothing."

"Thank you for the clothes, Miss Marilee. If you don't mind, I'd like to keep them here so that they don't get misplaced or taken. Some people at the mission get desperate and dishonest."

"That's perfectly fine with me," she says. "I'll wash them for you when I do the aprons and the towels."

Miss Marilee is such a nice person. I can tell that she has a kind heart and is sincere.

"Will I be wearing an apron?" I ask her. I really want to look like I belong there along with everyone else.

"Only when you work the shampoo bowl," she answers. "Otherwise, you don't have to wear one unless you want one." She can see that I do. "You can grab one from the closet near the break room and keep it up front with you."

A couple of the stylists arrive and Miss Marilee introduces me as the newest member of the Crowning Glory staff, which really makes me feel good.

Their friendly demeanor makes me feel welcome.

I notice a picture of Divine Matthews-Hardison on the wall. I didn't notice it when I was there yesterday. "Does she come here to get her hair done?" I ask China wide-eyed.

"Yeah. Her mom is also one of our clients. Kylie, we have a lot of high-profile and celebrity clientele. There may be times when a reporter or someone will try to come into the salon. Don't respond to any of their questions—just get my mother."

"Okay," I reply. I can't believe that I'm actually working in the same beauty shop where Divine gets her hair done. Miss Marilee is big-time.

China shows me how to print a list of daily appointments per stylist and how to schedule future ones. As she's talking, a client arrives.

"She's here to see my mother," China states. "I'll let you check her in."

I follow her instructions.

"You're a quick learner," China says afterward. "That's good. We have them check in so that we keep a history of the services they receive. This way we don't have to guess when they got a retouch or a full perm. All of the stylists will tell you if we add any additional services, and you have to record them as well."

"I can do that," I say. "Do the clients pay y'all, or do they come up and pay me?"

"They'll pay you. Are you comfortable with that?"

I nod quickly. "I'm really good with math. I just didn't know if I was responsible for taking payments from the clients. I forgot to ask Miss Marilee yesterday."

China stays up front with me until her ten o'clock appointment arrives. I have four more clients arrive. As China watches, I get them checked in and notify the stylists that their appointments are waiting.

Processing payments is easy and runs smoothly. I'm actually having a good time. Mostly it is because I have a job, which means that I will be getting a weekly paycheck. Once I save some money, Miss Lucy and I can get an address. I'll get my first paycheck on Saturday. I'm so excited. She says that she has veteran benefits coming but can't get them until she has a place to live.

I plan to save every penny I can of my paycheck. I know that I have to buy some more pants and shirts for work—maybe two pairs of black pants and a couple of shirts. I'll then have four outfits and can rotate them.

Miss Marilee gives me a bus pass. "I don't want you worrying about getting to work."

I offer to pay her back, but she says, "I just want you to show up for work as scheduled, Kylie. That's all that I ask of you."

"I can do that," I promise.

Shortly after twelve, Rhyann walks into the salon. "Kylie, what are you doing here?"

"Miss Marilee gave me a job. I'm the receptionist." I nervously check her reaction. "You didn't want the job, did you?" The last thing I want to do is betray the girl who has been so nice to me.

A wave of relief washes over me when Rhyann shakes her head. "I like washing hair and being in the back. I'd be bored to death sitting up here waiting for the phone to ring or having to deal with the money. I only like touching my own dollars."

I don't want Rhyann getting it twisted, so I say, "It's a job and I'm happy to have one, so I'll do whatever I have to do."

"Kylie, I'm so glad you're here," Rhyann tells me, a big grin on her face. "We can get to know each other better."

"Thanks for telling Miss Marilee that I needed my hair washed and stuff. I wouldn't have this job if it wasn't for you."

"Girl, it wasn't me—it was you. Miss Marilee knows good people when she sees them. So do I."

Her words thrill me.

Rhyann goes off to work, and China comes to relieve me.

"We ordered pizza for everyone," she tells me. "Go on to the break room and grab a couple of slices, Kylie. If you wait until the others get to it, there won't be anything left."

I chuckle.

"There's some soda in the fridge. We keep coffee, bottled water, soda, and snacks stocked for the staff and the clients. Mama sometimes brings in her homemade lemon cake or sour cream pound cake."

"I brought in some fruit," I say. "It's two apples and two oranges."

"You can keep them in the fridge with the other fruit or in a bag with your name on it."

"It looks like everybody shares, so I don't mind sharing."

She approves of this spirit. "We're a team, Kylie. We function as a unit, and that is why I believe the shop is so successful. You'll see that we all genuinely care for one another."

"I'll eat quickly, because I know that you have a one thirty appointment."

China breaks into a smile. "Take your time, Kylie. We don't want you choking or anything, okay?"

I'm still not sure. "I just don't want to mess around and be late. I don't want to lose my job before the ink is dry on my paperwork."

China laughs. "Just relax, Kylie. You're fine."

I walk to the back of the salon and into the break room. Rhyann joins me a few minutes later. We each get two slices of pepperoni pizza and sit down at the table.

"They bought out the Pizza Joint," Rhyann says. "I love pizza days. I usually eat at least four or five slices."

I eye the stack of pizza boxes. "They sure bought a lot of them. Do you think I can have one more slice?"

"Gurl, they'd be insulted if you didn't," Ryann responds. "Eat up. We've got a busy day ahead."

Rhyann was right. After lunch, we are busy with clients everywhere. Before I even realize it, my workday is over.

Rhyann and I walk to the bus stop together.

"I hate riding public transportation," she groans.

"I'm not a fan of it, either," I confess. "But it's the only way I can get anywhere."

Rhyann looks impatiently down the street. "I can't wait to get a car."

I glance over at Rhyann and inquire, "When are you getting one?"

"Hopefully, sometime this summer," she responds. "My aunt says that it's going to be a graduation present, but I'm trying to talk her down."

Rhyann's bus comes first.

"I'll see you tomorrow."

"Okay," I murmur and wave as she disappears on the bus. Mine shows up five minutes later.

Just as she promised, Miss Lucy is waiting for me.

"You feeling any better?" I ask her.

She nods. "Much better. Praise the Lord for His healing power."

When we sit down to eat dinner in the dining hall thirty minutes later, Miss Lucy asks, "So how was your first day on the job?"

"It was good," I respond between bites. "Everybody in the salon was real nice to me. China—that's Miss Marilee's daughter—is just as nice as her mother is. She told me that she would braid my hair again if I want it, but I should wait for about a month and not get a perm. I think I'm gonna stay away from braids for now."

I tear off a piece of my roll and stick it in my mouth. After I swallow, I say, "You should come meet Miss Marilee. You would like her. She was nice enough to make sure I had some clothes to work in, and she even gave me a bus pass."

"I believe that I will, Kylie. She sounds like a nice lady."

I lean toward Miss Lucy and whisper, "I made five dollars in tips today. I washed this lady's hair and she gave me five dollars."

"Did you have anything to eat besides the fruit you took with you?"

I nod. "They ordered pizza for the staff. I think Miss Marilee was concerned that I didn't have any money for lunch, so this was her way of making sure that I ate something. They keep soda and snacks in the break room for staff and the clients. Miss Marilee gives the clients fruit, muffins, cake . . . you name it. She's special, and that's why all her clients love her."

"I know that's right." Miss Lucy tries to smile, but suddenly she wipes her brow with a napkin.

"Are you okay?" I inquire. She just doesn't really seem like herself to me. I've got to find a way to get Miss Lucy to a doctor.

She nods.

"Miss Lucy, I can tell that you don't look like you're feeling well. What's wrong?"

I worry about Miss Lucy, and I don't want to lose her—she's all I have right now. I don't know how kids survive on these streets. It scares me to death.

"Miss Lucy, please tell me what's wrong?" I plead.

She takes my hand in hers. "I'm just tired, baby. I have these days when I'm so tired that it hurts to move. I have this long-lasting pain and tenderness in my muscles, joints, and tendons from time to time. I have a condition called fibromyalgia on top of my scoliosis."

"So what can be done about it?"

She sticks a forkful of rice into her mouth, chewing thoughtfully.

"There isn't a cure for it," Miss Lucy says. "But there are meds that can ease the pain. I probably need some PT, too."

"PT? What's that?" I ask.

"Physical therapy," Miss Lucy answers.

"Then we need to get the medicine," I state. "We'll get them when I get paid."

Miss Lucy shakes her head. "Kylie, I want you to save

your money. The meds I need is too expensive. I'll be fine, honey."

"We're a team," I say. "If you need medicine, then I'm gonna get you some. I don't want anything to happen to you."

She embraces me. "I'm not going anywhere, Kylie. I just ache from time to time, but God gives me the strength to go on. When it starts to get bad, I just say over and over again 'By Jesus' stripes, I'm healed.' That's what the word of God says, and I believe it."

I let the matter drop for now, but I intend to get the medicine that will help Miss Lucy. It's the least I can do for all she's done for me.

She eyes me before saying, "I know what you're thinking. Kylie, I'm telling you that I want you to save your money. We are gonna get into one of those transitional houses so that you can get back into school and I can go after my veteran benefits. See, I have a plan for myself."

"But until you get your benefits, let me help you."

Miss Lucy shakes her head. "I'll be fine. God is going to take good care of me until I can get to the VA hospital."

I pray silently that she is right. I have already lost my grandmother and my mama. I do not want to lose another person. I can't handle another loss.

Chapter 4

"Kylie, where are you living?" Miss Marilee inquires the next day while we are cleaning up for the evening. "Are you still staying at one of the missions, or have you been able to move into a shelter?" She has waited until we're the only two left in the shop besides China and her husband. He's the police officer people have seen hanging around.

"Yes, ma'am," I respond, sweeping up the hair and other debris from the floor. "I'm staying at the Safe Harbor Mission."

"I hate the thought of you being out here all alone with no family. I'm surprised you haven't been placed in foster care."

"I want to be emancipated. Now that I have a job, I can get the process started."

She was thinking along different lines, though. "I've been thinking about your situation, and I might have something for you. I have an empty studio apartment available in a building I own on Sixth Street. You can have it if you want."

I stop sweeping. "How much is the rent?"

"It will be considered part of your salary."

I can't believe my good luck, yet I have to think for two now. "Miss Marilee, can I have someone stay there with me?" I ask. "There's this woman—her name is Miss Lucy and she's been watching over me on the streets. She is real sick, although she doesn't think that I know it. I just don't feel right just leaving her alone after everything she's done for me."

"I'd like to meet her first," Miss Marilee responds, "before I give you an answer."

I hate to make things hard, but I have to tell her. "She gets tired a lot, and she doesn't like to ride the bus because of her back. It's not a comfortable ride for her."

After finishing her report, Miss Marilee takes the money out of the register and sticks it into a zippered pouch. "Then I'll just come to her. I'll give you a ride to the mission."

"She's most likely at the bus stop. She waits there for me

every day. Miss Lucy is very protective of me." I tell her about the way she went after Lucky D with a baseball bat to save me.

"She is a very brave woman," Miss Marilee replies. "We don't want her to worry, so I'll just stop by and pick her up, and then we'll head over to the apartment."

It's like a good angel has come into my life. "Miss Marilee, I can't thank you enough for all this stuff that you've done for me."

"Kylie, you are such a dear. I can see how hard you're working to build a life for yourself. Sometimes people need a helping hand."

"My grandma used to always talk about how people blessed her. Miss Marilee, you've really blessed me."

"I feel the same way about you."

We hop into her car and drive until I see Miss Lucy. "There she is."

We pull off the street into an empty parking space.

"Miss Lucy, this is Miss Marilee," I say as I step out of her car. "She's wanted to meet you because she offered me a studio apartment. She's gonna take us over there to see it."

"It's nice to meet you, Lucy," Miss Marilee says in greeting.

The two women are cordial to one another.

I get into the backseat of the Volvo so that they can talk and get to know each other. I pray that Miss Marilee will let me share the apartment with Miss Lucy. I've come to realize that I'm not ready to live alone.

"You look so familiar to me," Miss Marilee tells her. "I know you from somewhere."

"Yeah, I was thinking the same thing," Miss Lucy responds. "I was in the army for almost sixteen years."

"That's it," Miss Marilee says. "We met when my daughter graduated from high school—it's been about three years. I sat with you and your sister, and we talked about your military career. Your niece was graduating."

"That's right. Lydia graduated." Miss Lucy's smile disappears. "She and my sister died a month later in a car accident."

Miss Marilee is sympathetic. "I remember that. My daughter China attended the funeral."

Miss Lucy nods. "It took a toll on me, losing them both like that."

"How did you end up here?" Miss Marilee wants to know. "What happened?"

"I was depressed a lot, and I turned to alcohol to take the edge off," Miss Lucy confessed. "Then, as I prepared to deploy to the Persian Gulf, the army discovered I had scoliosis and gave me a medical discharge. I think we talked about that."

Miss Marilee nods in agreement. "You had just gotten a job, and you were very excited about it."

Miss Lucy sighs. "Well, it didn't last long. I was unable to sit or stand for long periods, so I couldn't keep a job too long. On top of that, I had a drinking problem. I later found out that I also have fibromyalgia. I've been out of work since 2000, on and off drugs for ten years, and last March I lost the apartment I've had since 2005."

Miss Marilee parked the car. "Have you seen a doctor about your scoliosis?"

Miss Lucy shakes her head. "There's not much a doctor can do for me for that. I can take meds for the fibromyalgia as soon as I get my benefits."

"I just don't think that she needs to be out on the streets in her condition," I blurt out. "Miss Marilee, she gets tired a lot, and some days she can hardly move."

"I agree with you, Kylie. The only thing I have available right now is the studio apartment, but perhaps we can put a sofa bed in there."

I nod in agreement. "Honestly, Miss Marilee, I don't mind sleeping on the floor as long as I have a roof over my head. Miss Lucy needs a real bed."

Miss Lucy holds up a hand in protest. "Marilee, you don't have to do this for me. The child really needs to get off the streets. I would feel better if I know that she's safe."

"As you mentioned, she is a child," Miss Marilee replies thoughtfully. "I think it's a good idea to have you there with her. She looks to you as her guardian. I think once you all are settled, it would be a good idea to make it legal, especially with her mother gone. I think it's better than Kylie trying to get emancipated."

I pray Miss Lucy doesn't say anything about my mama being alive and well.

"Would you like to see your new home?" Miss Marilee asks. "I had it cleaned this morning. You can move in today if you want. There is a queen-size bed in the apartment, and I'll bring over an air mattress. Kylie, you can use it until you get the sofa bed."

"Thank you, Marilee," Miss Lucy says. "May God continue to pour His blessings upon you for your kindness. God bless you."

"I wish the same for you," Miss Marilee responds. "It's a blessing for you to take care of a motherless child and protect her like you have."

She drives us over to West Sixth Street and parks in front of a building covered in peach-colored brick and stone. It's accented with an arched doorway, a cobblestone walkway lined by bright green grass, and colorful beds of flowers.

"This is nice," I murmur. My mama's building is not as clean or secure-looking as this one. I cannot wait to see the actual apartment, especially if the outside is so pretty.

We get out of the car and follow Miss Marilee inside.

"This is a beautiful building," Miss Lucy says. "Nice and clean."

"I do my best to keep it looking good. I know how I like to live," Miss Marilee comments. "I want the same for my tenants."

We take the elevator up to the second floor.

"Well, here we are," Miss Marilee says to us as she opens

the front door of apartment 204. "This is where you and Kylie will live."

I step aside to let Miss Lucy enter first.

I don't know about Miss Lucy, but I fall instantly in love with the huge, square, eggshell-colored apartment with hardwood floor, a small kitchen area, and a bathroom.

"There is a large walk-in closet," Miss Marilee points out. "I believe it's big enough for the two of you to share for now."

Miss Lucy and I agree. It's not like we have a lot of clothes. Neither one of us has much of anything.

A nice four-poster bed sits against the back wall.

"That bed is pretty," I tell Miss Lucy.

"It sure is."

I turn to Miss Marilee and ask, "You're really gonna let us stay here in this beautiful apartment? I know you say this is part of my salary, but aren't you losing money?"

"I'm not losing money, Kylie. I value my employees, and I want to be fair to them. Lisa lives in apartment 208 just down the hall. Some days you might be able to ride to work with her."

Lisa works in Crowning Glory and is really nice. I like knowing that we have a friendly face in the building.

I hug Miss Marilee. "I promise we won't mess up this pretty apartment. We're gonna keep it nice and clean."

"I have no doubt that you will," she responds with a smile. "I'm going to go pick up some things for you two. I'll be back in a little while." Miss Marilee walks to the front door. "Oh, what would you like to eat?"

"It doesn't matter to me," I say. I'm just happy to have a roof over my head and not having to stand in line in hopes of getting a bed for the night. I still plan on going back to the mission to help out from time to time, but I never want to have to stay there again.

"How about Chinese food?" Miss Marilee suggests. "Sweet and sour chicken, fried rice, and egg rolls?"

"That's fine," Miss Lucy and I say in unison.

"I'll be back in a little while." She smiles. "Make yourself comfortable. This is your new home."

"Miss Lucy, we got us a place to live," I announce, dancing around the small apartment. "We stepping in high cotton now."

"Ain't that the truth?" Miss Lucy's eyes travel the room. "This place is so nice and clean, too. Marilee is not like some landlords I've dealt with in the past—she keeps her building spotless."

"We don't have to worry about beds or standing in those long lines to take showers anymore."

"Praise the Lord for what He has done," Miss Lucy cries. "We are truly blessed." She begins walking around the apartment chanting a prayer. She always says that you can't thank God enough. I don't want to seem ungrateful, so I start thanking Him, too.

Miss Marilee returns forty-five minutes later with food.

"I went by Target to pick up some sheets and towels. I left them in the car. We can bring them upstairs after we eat."

"Thank you so much, Miss Marilee," I say as she hands me a paper plate. "I can't ever repay you for all this. I don't know what I'd do without you."

"I just give thanks to my Heavenly Father above for blessing me so that I can be a blessing to others."

We take our plates and sit down at the table near the kitchen.

Miss Lucy says a prayer before we eat.

"I ate so much of this when I was pregnant with China. That's how she got her name," Miss Marilee tells us with a chuckle.

"For real?" I ask.

She nods. "I thought I was having a boy, so I didn't have any names for a girl picked out."

I really like Miss Marilee. Sometimes, I wish that I had her or Miss Lucy for a mom or that my mama was more like them instead of acting like a hoochie.

I can't remember a time when my mama ever helped me with homework or even asked how school was going. She barely paid any attention to my report cards. The truth is that I could have signed her name to them without letting her see them. She never asked to see my grades. What parent doesn't want to see their son or daughter's grades?

Humph! If I decided I wanted to stay home from school, my mama was cool with it. Mama was never abusive to me, but she just never put me first in her life. Her men were her priority.

Miss Marilee's words cut into my thoughts. "I'm going to take you two grocery shopping and get you a starter set for the kitchen. There are some towels and sheets for the bed in my car. Now, before you try to give me your first paycheck back, Kylie—this is my gift to you and Lucy. Consider them housewarming presents. Okay?"

I give in. "Yes, ma'am."

She and Miss Lucy talk while I go down to Miss Marilee's car for the bag of stuff she brought over for us.

I hum softly, tapping my foot to the melody as I wait for the elevator doors to open. When they do, I step inside and press the button for the lobby.

Her car is right out front. I unlock the doors, retrieve the shopping bag, and make sure that I lock up her car before heading back into the building.

I pause a moment and smile as I eye the mailbox, a huge grin on my face—a mailbox that belongs to Miss Lucy and me.

We have an address.

Chapter 5

The woman getting out of the black Ford Explorer across the street from the shop propels me out of my chair.

I come from behind the counter and walk briskly across the floor to the huge picture window in order to get a better look. My suspicions are correct.

It's *her.*

My mama is just across the street, going into a shop with the man I'm assuming is Clyde, her new boyfriend.

The familiar tightness settles in my chest and I feel dizzy as I struggle to breathe. I begin to pant, gasping for air.

Miss Marilee surveys my face and rushes to my side. "Kylie, what's wrong?"

"C-can't breathe . . ."

She leads me over to a nearby chair in the reception area. The attack passes, much to my relief.

"Honey, are you okay?" Miss Marilee asks. "What's going on?"

"I have these attacks sometimes," I say in a low voice. "My chest gets real tight and I can't breathe." A lone tear rolls down my cheek. "I hate it because I always feel like I'm gonna die. All I know is that it scares me, Miss Marilee. I don't like feeling this way."

"It sounds like you had a panic attack," Miss Marilee tells me, giving me a hug. "Have you ever been diagnosed?"

"No, ma'am," I respond. "I didn't know that I could."

"How long have you had them?"

"Since my mama . . ."

Miss Marilee gives me an understanding nod. "We need to get you in to see a doctor. Maybe he can help you by giving you some meds or something. How often do you get them?"

"When I'm under a lot of stress or feel scared, they happen more often. I thought that maybe I was losing it or dying. That's what it feels like to me."

"You're going to be fine, Kylie. We just have to find a way

for you to handle the attacks when they happen. However, I'm going to pray for your healing. The Bible says that by Jesus' stripes we are healed. You have faith that God's word is true and hold on to that promise."

"You sound like Miss Lucy now. She always tells me that."

"It's true. God can take those attacks away from you."

"I hope that He'll do that," I say. "I don't want to be scared no more, Miss Marilee. I was scared all the time even before . . ." I stop short before I say something about my supposedly dead mama.

My eyes stray to the window. My mama's car is parked across the street. From the looks of things, she might be over there for a time.

"Why don't you step outside for a little while to get some fresh air?" Miss Marilee suggests.

"No, ma'am," I say a little too quickly. "I feel fine now. I need to get back to work."

"Are you sure?"

"Miss Marilee, I've wasted too much time already. It's better for me to do this sooner than in a while."

"If you're sure," Miss Marilee says with a smile.

I make my way back up to the reception desk, silently praying that my mama will stay across the street or, better yet, find another block to haunt. I hope she isn't of the mind-set to get her hair done.

If she were to walk into Crowning Glory, I would just die

right here on the spot. As Grandma Ellen used to say, I'd be no earthly good.

She bounces out of the shop across the street carrying two shopping bags. I guess Clyde must have some benjamins, because I know my mama can't afford to shop like that with no job.

I hold my breath when it looks like she's about to come across the street, heading straight to the salon. Clyde checks his watch and tells her something. Whatever it is, it causes her to change direction and head back to her car.

They get inside and drive off.

"Thank you, Jesus," I whisper. The last thing I need is my mama coming in here and acting all ghetto. If she had any idea that I worked here, she'd be here all the time trying to get money and free services.

On Sunday, Miss Lucy and I attend church with Miss Marilee and her daughter. China's baby girl is so cute, and she doesn't cry when I hold her.

I'm stricken with guilt as I sit here beside the two people who have been nothing but nice to me.

Lord, please don't strike me down for lying to Miss Marilee. I feel terrible about it and I want to tell her the truth—I just don't want to lose my job or the apartment, so please don't let her ever find out.

Sitting here in church only makes me feel like the worst

person in the world. A girl like me has no right to be in the house of the Lord. I'm a liar.

Miss Lucy looks over and smiles at me.

I smile weakly back.

I raise my eyes heavenward and pray for forgiveness. I try to convince myself that God knows my heart and He knows why I lied in the first place. I even try to convince myself that He will forgive me since I'm basically not a bad person. I've lived by most of the Ten Commandments—at least the ones that apply to my life.

I have what my grandma calls a healthy fear of the Lord, so I tried to turn down Miss Marilee's invitation to church, but Miss Lucy really wanted to come. She said that she was in desperate need of a word from the Lord. There was no way I would deprive her of that, so here I am, sitting here in church with a big L on my forehead.

It's not like I want to be a liar. I just don't know how to tell Miss Marilee and China the truth. I really don't want them to hate me.

I shift uncomfortably in the pew, hoping that the good Lord doesn't decide to strike me down. I can't wait for church to let out—my nerves are going all kinds of crazy.

"What was going on with you during the service?" Miss Lucy asks as soon as we reach our apartment a couple of hours later. "And you hardly touched your food during lunch."

"I feel so guilty for lying to Miss Marilee," I confess.

"Look at everything she's done for us, and how do I repay her? I tell one heck of a whopper."

"Kylie, why don't you just tell Marilee the truth about your mother? She would understand. This woman cares a great deal for you."

"Miss Lucy, I don't want to lose my job or for us to lose our home." I start to cry. "If she finds out I lied to her, we'll lose e-everything, and we got it good r-right now."

She hugs me. "Marilee isn't gonna put us out. I don't believe she would do that. It's not too late to go to her and be honest about what happened between you and your mother."

I wipe my face with the back of my hand. "You don't think she'll be mad?"

Miss Lucy shakes her head. "I don't, honey. She just may want to know why you didn't tell her the truth from the beginning. That's what I'd do if it was me."

The telephone rings.

I answer it. "Hello."

"Hi, Kylie, it's me, Rhyann."

"Hey, girl," I say. "What are you up to?"

Out of the corner of my eye, I see Miss Lucy navigate to her bed and take a seat on the edge to remove her shoes.

"Nothing," Rhyann responds. "I was calling to see if you have any plans for today?"

"No. Miss Lucy and I are just sitting here talking," I say. "Why, what do you have in mind?"

"Well, if you're up for some company, I was thinking of coming over. I thought that maybe we could just talk or watch a movie. The only time I really see you is when we're working."

I break into a grin. "Rhyann, I would love it. When can you get here?"

"How about two o'clock?"

"That's perfect," I reply. "See you then."

After hanging up the phone, I turn around to face Miss Lucy. "Rhyann's coming for a visit."

I'm excited about having a visitor. I miss my friends in North Carolina and want to find some girls here in L.A. to spend time with and just hang out.

"That's good. It's about time you started spending time with some girls your age."

In my own selfishness, I forgot to consider if she felt up for company. "Miss Lucy, I'm so sorry. I should've asked if you were okay with it."

"It's fine, Kylie," Miss Lucy assures me. "I can't wait to meet Rhyann. Do you think she'll want to stay for dinner?"

"We can ask her," I respond. "Thanks, Miss Lucy." I get up and go wash my face, then check out the apartment to make sure there's not a speck of dust to be found. I don't want Rhyann to find our home dirty.

When she arrives an hour later, I introduce Rhyann to Miss Lucy and proudly show off our new apartment.

"The lady across the hall was going to put this sofa in the

dump, but Miss Lucy asked her if we could have it and she said yeah. We didn't know it was a sofa bed at the time, but it is. This is where I sleep. We're going to put a sheet over it for now until we can find a sofa cover."

Rhyann surveys it a moment, then says, "To be honest, Kylie, it doesn't really look bad. I can't believe she was gonna throw that sofa away. I would've snatched it up, too."

"It sleeps well," I agree. "It's better than a cardboard box any day or the futon I used to have to sleep on when I was with my mama."

Rhyann drops down on the sofa. "Girl, I can't sleep on those things either. I had a futon but ended up giving it to my sister to put in her guest room."

I sit down beside her. "I'm glad you were able to come over. You're my first visitor outside of Miss Marilee."

While we're chatting, Miss Lucy is over in the kitchen cooking up our Sunday dinner.

"It smells delicious over there," I say. "Miss Lucy, you working it out."

She laughs. "Rhyann, are you staying for dinner? There's more than enough for me and Kylie. We'll be eating on this gospel bird for two or three days."

Rhyann chuckles, and I explain, "Miss Lucy calls chicken the gospel bird. Her pastor showed up every time her mama cooked chicken."

"I'd love to have dinner with you and Kylie. That food is smelling real good, especially the gospel bird. I only had a bagel for breakfast this morning and some chips on the way over here." Rhyann pulls out her cell phone. "Let me call my cousin and tell him not to come pick me up until around eight."

I glance over at Miss Lucy and smile.

When the food is ready, we gather around the small table to eat our dinner.

Rhyann is so funny, and I really enjoy her company. I like that she is so down to earth and isn't ashamed of going to a fancy school on scholarship or living near the jungle.

"So you really like going to Stony Hills Prep?" I ask. "The other girls, they don't treat you differently?"

Rhyann shakes her head. "They treat me fine. I've made some great friends there. I love all of my classes except Physics. That's my least favorite one. Latin is just okay. My favorite classes are English and World History."

"Math and Science are my favorite classes," I say. "If I could've stayed in school, I would be on the honor roll."

"Now that you have this apartment, you can go back to school," Rhyann points out. She wipes her mouth on the edge of the napkin.

"That's what I plan to do," I respond. "Now that I have a place to live, I can enroll in high school. I already know that I'll probably have to repeat tenth grade, but I'm okay with that. I'll do whatever I have to do."

Miss Lucy finishes off her dinner roll before saying, "Marilee's gonna help Kylie get back in school, and she's gonna see if she can take some extra classes so that she'll be able to graduate on time."

"Do you know what school you'll be going to?" Rhyann asks.

"Belmont High," I reply. "I heard that it was a pretty decent school."

"I wish you could attend Stony Hills with me."

The very idea shocks me. "Rhyann, I couldn't afford to go to the office in that place. I saw the campus on the news one time. It looks really expensive."

"It's definitely not cheap," she tells me. "But there are scholarships. I wouldn't be there without one."

After dinner, Rhyann helps me clean the kitchen even though I tell her that it's not necessary.

When we finish, we settle down on the sofa and watch television. Miss Lucy got money from her military retirement and used some of it to buy us a nice television from a store that was going out of business.

"I'm so glad you came over today," I tell Rhyann.

"Thanks for letting me visit," she responds. "You're cool, Kylie. You just went up five notches on my friend chart."

I laugh.

Her cousin Chester comes to pick her up shortly after eight. I walk down to the first floor with her.

"I'll see you on Tuesday," Rhyann tells me.

She walks outside where her cousin is waiting on her. He sees me and waves.

I wave back.

When she's gone, I head back up to the second floor.

Miss Lucy is in the shower when I return. I pick up the remote control and surf channels, searching for something she and I will both enjoy. Since there's only one television, we try to compromise.

Sometimes, I just let her watch TV while I read or listen to music. I bought myself an inexpensive MP3 player.

Life can't get any better than this, as far as I'm concerned.

Chapter 6

When Tuesday arrives, I'm more than ready to get back to work.

Miss Lucy and I spent most of yesterday at the Veteran's Administration office checking on all of her benefits. Things are working out and she is going to get everything she's entitled to, but it was a pretty long day, meeting with this person and that person.

Rhyann and I are working the same shift today, so we

have lunch together. While we are at the deli down the street, her cell phone rings.

When I hear her mention Divine's name, I can barely eat for trying to listen to her conversation.

She can't be talking to Divine Matthews-Hardison.

Can she?

When I hear her mention an upcoming movie with Kara, I can barely contain my excitement. Rhyann is sitting here talking to Divine. She's really talking to my role model. WOW!

"I wasn't trying to listen to your conversation, but you really know Divine Matthews-Hardison like that?" I say when she gets off the phone. "You two are friends like that?"

Rhyann shrugs. "She's like my best friend. We've been friends for a while now."

"That's so cool," I say. "She's in all of the fashion magazines with her mom. They seem to have a great relationship."

"They do," Rhyann responds. "Dee and Miss Kara are really close. Every summer they take this girls' retreat to some exotic island. They always take Alyssa—she's Dee's cousin. They're coming home this week, and I can't wait. We always have a great time together."

"Dee?"

"Oh yeah, I call her Dee." Rhyann bites into her sandwich.

"A mother and daughter should be closer than close, I feel."

Nodding, Rhyann agrees with me. "If my mom had lived, I think we would be like that."

I don't respond.

I love my mom, and my deepest wish is that she loved me half as much. I wish that she loved me enough to focus on me. Why can't I be enough for her? At least until I can handle my own life.

"Kylie, did you hear what I said?" Rhyann asks, bringing me out of my reverie.

"Huh?" I utter. "I'm sorry. What were you saying?"

"I asked you about school. Have you decided to go back?"

"Yeah, but I'm probably gonna have to repeat my tenth grade year."

"Maybe not," Rhyann replies. "You could probably test out of some of your classes. I can help you if you want. We can prepare you over the summer."

That's such a generous thing to offer. "I've never had a friend like you."

She smiles. "I've never had a friend quite like you, either. I like how you're so down to earth. You're not caught up in being a fashionista or a diva—it's refreshing. Don't get me wrong. I love my girls, Mimi and Divine, but they—"

I cut her off by asking, "You and Mimi Reuben are friends, too? How did you get to know them? Is it because you work at the beauty shop?"

Rhyann chuckles. "Kylie, we call them hair salons out here."

"A horse is a horse no matter how fancy you try to make

the name," I respond. "Tarjae is still Target when all's said and done. *It is what it is.*"

Rhyann laughs. "You're right about that. Now I see why you and Miss Lucy get along so well. You sound just like her with some of the stuff you say."

"We're both Southern," I answer proudly.

After we finish eating, we head back to the salon, laughing and talking like longtime friends.

"You need to let me take you home," some dude shouts out as we walk by.

"Who is he talking to?" I ask.

Rhyann gives me a sidelong glance. "You."

"Humph," I grunt. "I wouldn't give him air if he were in a jug."

She howls with laughter. "Kylie, where do you come up with this stuff?"

"My Grandma Ellen," I tell her.

"My boo is picking me up tonight. I can't wait for you to meet him," Rhyann tells me as she throws her cup in a nearby trash can.

"How long have you been together?"

"Not too long," Rhyann answers. "He's going off to college this fall. He'll be going to N.C. State."

"That's great," I say. "That's such a cool school. I'd planned to go there when I was younger."

"Did you have a boyfriend before everything happened?"

I meet Rhyann's gaze and respond, "No. I never really

had one. I've had lots of male friends, but nothing like a boyfriend."

"Well, you're not going to have any trouble finding one," Rhyann confirms. "Watch and see. You're going to have so many boys coming at you."

"To be honest with you, Rhyann, I'm not even thinking about boys. I have to get my life straight, you know? I need to graduate high school so that I can go to college. I have to be able to take care of myself."

"I know exactly what you mean. I felt the same way. But you do know that we're only young once in a lifetime. We have to enjoy our lives. Before you came to work at the salon, there was this client—her name was Mrs. Goldberg. She was my friend." Rhyann's voice breaks as she talks. "She died not too long ago, but before she passed on, Mrs. G made me promise to live my life without regret. Kylie, I'm saying the same thing to you."

"I heard China and Miss Marilee mention her," I say. "I can tell how much you all miss her."

"You would've liked her a lot, Kylie."

Once we walk through the doors of the Crowning Glory Salon, it's back to work. Three people in the reception area are waiting to be taken back to the shampoo bowl. I make sure that they have been checked in on the computer.

I love my job.

೦೦

I have my hair in kinky twists today, and I have on a new pair of blue jeans from Walmart with a nice Old Navy shirt that I couldn't resist purchasing. I waited patiently until it was on sale so that I wouldn't feel guilty when I bought it.

Divine is arriving today, and she is supposed to come by the beauty shop to check in with Rhyann.

The past couple of days, I have been so excited about finally meeting her. She was in Antigua for the past two weeks vacationing with her mother and her cousin. Rhyann says that they do this every year, and not even Kevin Nash is allowed. I think that's pretty cool. She puts her daughter *and* her niece first at times.

"You look so cute," Rhyann tells me when I arrive for work. "Who are you all dressed up for?"

"I'm not dressed up," I say.

A black Lincoln Town Car slows to a stop in front of the salon.

"They're here," Rhyann says. "Divine and Alyssa just pulled up."

Divine gets out of the car, her long hair blowing in the wind. She looks great in her designer jeans with matching jacket and silver sandals. Her cousin looks a lot like her, I note.

Rhyann runs out of the shop to give them both hugs. They must really be close friends, I decide.

Rhyann enthusiastically introduces me to Divine. "This is my friend Kylie. She works here now."

"Hey," Divine says. "Nice to meet you."

"I've heard a lot about you," I gush. "I'm glad to finally meet you. I—"

She smiles, then excuses herself to go talk to Miss Marilee.

Her cousin walks over to where we're standing and says, "My name is Alyssa. What's your name?"

"I'm Kylie."

"It's nice to meet you. I heard Rhyann say that you two were friends. I hope we'll get to hang out this summer."

I steal a peek over at Divine before replying, "I hope so, too."

Although I try to hide it, my feelings are hurt by Divine's abrupt dismissal of me. I couldn't wait to meet her, and she barely gives pea turkey squat. Her cousin is much nicer.

I look down at my clothes. They're clean and everything, but they do shout that I'm a Walmart preferred shopper, while Divine has probably never seen the inside of one. There is no reason she should want to be my friend. Even though I know this, my feelings are still raw.

Divine and Alyssa don't stay long because they have a few more stops to make. I know that Rhyann will be seeing them later on, because I overheard them make plans. I wish Rhyann or Alyssa had thought to include me, but they did not, so oh well.

Defeated, I decide that I will never be a normal teenager. I will never have a mother to love me, and I will never have a circle of friends like Rhyann has in Divine, Mimi, and Alyssa.

"What's wrong, Kylie?" Rhyann asks me after they leave.

"Nothing," I respond glumly.

"C'mon, I know something's up," she tells me. "You were so excited about meeting Divine. Now you look like you're about to cry."

"I'm not about to do no crying. I met Divine, and she is not what I thought she was. That's all."

"What do you mean by that?"

"I guess you didn't see the way she stared me down when you introduced us. She hardly spoke and then walked off."

"I don't think she meant any harm by it," Rhyann says, defending her. "She's tired from flying, and trust me on this—she's not the friendliest person when she's tired."

"I don't think she liked me."

"Kylie, she doesn't know you. It was just the first meeting. You'll see . . . Dee's going to put you on her B.F.F. list before the summer ends."

I frown. "List? She has a list?"

Rhyann laughs. "It's just a saying, Kylie. There's no real list—at least I don't think she has one. You can never tell with Dee."

"It's fine if she doesn't want to be my friend," I say. "Her cousin Alyssa was real nice to me, though."

Rhyann breaks into a grin. "She's Southern, too."

"GRITS have it going on," I respond.

"Girl, why you talking about grits? Are you hungry?"

I laugh. "Not grits, Rhyann. I'm talking about G-R-I-T-S. It means 'girls raised in the South.'"

"Okaay. I like that."

I smile.

"Seriously, Kylie, you don't have to worry about Divine. She is going to like you as much as I do."

I'm not so sure, but I let the matter drop. If Divine doesn't want to be my friend, I'll still be fine.

When I get home, I tell Miss Lucy, "I met Divine today."

"How did it go? I know how excited you were about meeting her."

"I don't think she liked me," I say. "Rhyann says that she was just tired from traveling, but I don't know. Her cousin was nice, though."

Miss Lucy drains her pasta, then places it back on the stove. "Well, Rhyann could be right."

"She wasn't rude to anyone else," I say. "To be honest, Divine wasn't exactly rude to me—she just wasn't interested in talking to me. She talked to Miss Marilee and China, and then she made plans with Rhyann. She and Alyssa left after that."

Miss Lucy stirred the spaghetti sauce. "You wanted to be included, didn't you?"

"I've always admired her. It is not like I want her life or anything. She just seemed like a nice person in the pictures I have seen in the magazines. I just thought it would be nice to get to know someone like her. Her parents had some drama, but she seems like she's dealt with it well. I guess I felt like she could relate to what I'm going through."

"I'm sure you'll see her again. Just see what happens."

The next day, Divine shows up at the salon while I'm in the back putting away a new order of supplies.

"What is she doing here?" I ask in a low whisper.

"She must have a hair appointment," Rhyann responds matter-of-factly. "Go on up and check her in. I need to rinse China's client."

The last thing I want to do right now is deal with the diva.

Biting my lip, I walk up to the receptionist area to greet her, since it's my job. Before I can open my mouth, she smiles and says, "Kylie, hey . . . I have an appointment with China."

I return her smile. "She'll be with you shortly."

I wait for her to walk away from the counter, but she doesn't. Instead, she says, "I didn't get a chance to really talk to you yesterday. We had just gotten in, and I wanted to stop by here to see Rhyann and book my hair appointment."

Putting a hand to her hair, she says, "I know you can tell that I need a serious perm. I was so tired. Alyssa told me that I might have offended you, and I want to apologize. I didn't mean it."

"We're cool," I say. I'm touched that she thinks enough

of me to say she's sorry. As for Alyssa, she's at the top of my friend list, right under Rhyann. That's if I had a list.

"I've heard some really nice things about you from my girl," Divine is saying. "We used to be the fabulous four, but I see now that we're going to have to become the fab five. That sounds better anyway."

I laugh. "Naw, I think y'all will still be the fabulous four. There's nothing fab about me."

"Well, you could use a few fashion tips," Divine says, checking out my outfit. "I know that we're just getting to know each other, so please understand that I don't mean what I just said in a bad way, Kylie. If you are beautiful on the inside, that beauty will even shine in a paper bag. That's what my Aunt Phoebe says all the time."

"She sounds like my Grandma Ellen. She talked like that."

"Where are you from?"

"Statesville, North Carolina. I sound country, huh?"

Divine dismisses my words with a wave of her hand. "I live in the country, so don't even sweat it. I like your accent," Divine responds. "Rhyann's always telling me that I sound Southern now."

"That's because you do," she says from behind me. "C'mon, Diva. I need to shampoo you."

Before Divine leaves, she tells me, "Kylie, I'll talk to you in a few."

I meet Rhyann's gaze and grin.

"I told you," she mouths before following Divine to the back of the salon, where the shampoo bowls are located.

I seat my client in the chair beside Divine to shampoo her hair. While I'm working, I can hear her conversation with Rhyann.

"So are you and Madison talking at all?" Rhyann asks.

"Not really," Divine answers. "His baby is due in a few months, so I guess he's trying to deal with all that."

I can't help but wonder who they're talking about, but I turn my attention back to my client's head as I prepare to rinse her.

When I'm done with my client, I place her under the dryer per Miss Marilee's instructions. When the timer goes off, I'll rinse the conditioner out of her hair and take her to Miss Marilee.

China has been teaching Rhyann and me the proper way to roll a client's hair, but right now we only work with mannequin heads.

Divine takes a seat in China's chair.

When we're between clients, Rhyann and I take a few minutes to chat with Divine and China. I mostly just listen.

The telephone rings. I take off to answer it and end up staying up front because more clients venture in, including a couple of walk-ins. When Rhyann gets backed up at the shampoo bowl, I give her assistance.

When China is done with Divine's hair, she comes to the front desk to pay for her services. While I ring her up, she says, "Kylie, we're all going to the beach on Sunday after church. Would you like to go with us?"

I'm totally surprised by her invitation. Divine actually asked me to accompany her and her friends to the beach? This is like a dream come true.

"Kylie," she prompts. "Did you hear me?"

I swallow hard. "I'm sorry, I . . . you caught me off guard. Are you sure you want me to come with y'all?"

Divine gives a slight nod. "Why wouldn't I?"

I don't respond that I'm not like them. I don't have a celebrity parent or a huge bank account.

She pays me in cash.

"I would love to join you all, but I don't have a car, Divine."

"We'll come pick you up," she responds. "Mimi has a car, and we're picking up Rhyann, so we can get you, too."

"I don't live near Rhyann," I say. "Maybe I can meet you at her house, though. I'll check to see if that's okay."

"That's fine with me," Rhyann announces when she joins us in the reception area. "We're going to have so much fun."

I give a tight smile. I'm excited about spending time with Divine, Rhyann, and Alyssa, but this will be my first time meeting Mimi. I don't know how she's going to act around me, since I'm not really one of them.

Divine leaves the shop a few minutes later when her mother and Alyssa come to pick her up. I sneak a glimpse of Kara Matthews while she's sitting in the car chatting on her cell phone.

What am I thinking about? I don't belong around people like Divine and Mimi.

Just the thought of being around them makes my stomach quiver in anxiety.

Maybe I shouldn't go, I decide. I really don't have anything in common with those girls, despite the fact that I desperately want to be friends with them.

Chapter 7

D ivine came back to the beauty shop today," I announce cheerfully as soon as I walk into the apartment. "She even apologized for the way she treated me yesterday, Miss Lucy."

"That's real nice of her."

I nod in agreement. "I was so shocked. She's really cool, and she even invited me to go to the beach with them on Sunday after church. Do you mind if I go?"

Miss Lucy shakes her head. "Honey, you go on and have yourself a wonderful time. You need to spend time with other girls your own age."

"I'm going to take the bus to Rhyann's house, and Mimi, another one of their friends, gonna come and pick us up. Miss Lucy, I can't believe that I'm going to be hanging out with them. Mimi's dad is on that new show *Legend*."

"I like that show," Miss Lucy says. "Honey, I'm so happy you're finding friends."

"I really want them to like me."

"They will," Miss Lucy tells me. "You're a very likeable person, Kylie."

Deep down, I really hope Miss Lucy's right.

The next couple of days pass slowly. The closer we get to Sunday, the more nervous I become about spending time with Divine and Mimi. Rhyann and Alyssa are pretty normal, and I can relate to them, but the other two—they might think I'm nothing but street trash.

The other thing that bothers me is that I don't have a swimsuit. Miss Lucy told me that Walmart carries them, so I'm hoping to find something on sale. I don't want to be the odd girl out.

My stomach churns nervously every time I think about going to the beach. I can't believe that I'm actually going to kick it with Divine and Mimi. This is like the coolest thing ever.

I really want them to like me. I want so much to be a part

of their circle. No way I'd ever tell them this, though. Not even Rhyann.

This will be my little secret. That way I won't be disappointed if they don't want anything to do with the homeless girl.

I wish Sunday would just get here already.

After church, I take the bus to Rhyann's neighborhood.

She is at the bus stop waiting for me. "We're going to have so much fun today," Rhyann tells me. "I'm telling you now that Mimi and Divine are crazy. They may be divas, but they like to have fun."

"So they're pretty down to earth, then?"

Rhyann nods. "Yeah, they're cool. I wouldn't be dealing with them otherwise."

I relax a little while we walk to the next block, where Rhyann lives. She introduces me to her aunt and brothers.

"Your aunt's really nice," I say to Rhyann.

She agrees. "I don't know what I'd do without her. She took us in after my mom died. Auntie Mo gave up a lot to raise us and her own children."

Divine and Alyssa come with Mimi to pick us up.

Rhyann introduces me to Mimi, who says, "I've heard a lot of nice stuff about you. Welcome to our little group."

I smile.

We grab our bags and head out to the car.

"I love the beach," Alyssa says after we get there. "I could stay out here all day long."

I agree.

Divine, Alyssa, and Mimi all have on really nice swimsuits with matching cover-ups. Rhyann's suit is similar to mine in design, which leads me to assume she purchased hers at Walmart or Target, too. At least she has a nice wraparound skirt for hers. I have an old T-shirt and a pair of basketball shorts over my swimsuit.

"Kylie, how long have you been in L.A.?" Divine asks me, breaking the silence.

"Almost a year," I respond, taking the hot pink tote bag off my shoulder. After seeing the nice fluffy beach towels the others have in their totes, I'm grateful for the towels Miss Marilee gave us. Mine isn't a beach towel, but it'll do.

Still, I can't help the wave of embarrassment that washes over me. As much as they seem to accept me, I know that they can't help but notice my cheap swimsuit, the bath towel, and plain flip-flops.

"Do you like it out here?" Alyssa wants to know. "I'd love to live in Los Angeles."

I shrug and respond, "It's actually okay, Alyssa. Sometimes I miss being in North Carolina, but I do like that there aren't any mosquitoes. Those things used to wear me out something awful. I definitely don't miss them."

Mimi pulls a bottle of water from her designer tote. "So, where do you go to school, Kylie?"

I have no idea what Rhyann told them about me, but I see no need to lie to them. "I used to go to Dorsey, but I didn't finish my last semester."

"You did? You went to Dorsey?" Rhyann asks. "My brother Brady goes there. He was the quarterback. That's not too far from where I live. I would be going there if I hadn't gotten a scholarship to Stony Hills Prep."

When I met him at Rhyann's house, I remembered having seen him around school. He is so cute with those dreadlocks. Of course, he didn't seem to remember me, but that's okay. Brady always had some girl up in his face. "I remember that he was real popular."

Rhyann nods in agreement. "Everybody knows that boy."

"Speaking of brothers," Mimi says, "mine is moving out here. He and his mother are having some issues, so Father suggested that he come live with us. Mother's not exactly thrilled, but she's not going to go against my father."

"I forgot you have a brother," Divine says. "You hardly ever mention him."

"My mother and his mother don't get along. She's still mad that my mother kind of stole him from her." She is annoyed. "Get over it already."

"Do you and your brother get along?" Alyssa asks.

"We're cool," Mimi responds. "But then I've never really lived with Chandler for longer than a week or two."

"When is he coming?" Divine asks.

"My dad is flying to New York this evening. He and Chandler will be back on Tuesday."

"How old is he?" Rhyann wants to know.

"He's seventeen. This is going to be his last year in high school."

"I haven't told them anything about your situation," Rhyann tells me as she straightens out her towel on the sand. "I thought you should be the one to do that."

"What situation?" Divine asks. "Are you pregnant?"

I shake my head. "No, up until a few weeks ago, I was homeless, so it was hard to stay in school. That's why I didn't get to finish."

All of them were shocked. "Rhyann told me that you lost your parents, but I just assumed that you lived with a relative," Mimi says. "Kylie, I had no idea. We have plenty of room if you need somewhere to stay." She pulls out her cell phone. "I'll call Mother right now."

"You don't have to do that," I interject quickly. "You have your brother moving in. Besides, I have a home now. Miss Lucy and I live in a studio apartment in Miss Marilee's building. It's part of my salary."

I'm truly touched by Mimi's offer to have me come live with them. It's sweet, but I know that it would only be a temporary fix, and I am not looking for one of those. I want a home that nobody will ever be able to make me leave. I've been kicked out of way too many places already.

My mama and her brother sold Grandma Ellen's house

and split what was left after her bills were paid. That's what my mama used to buy her SUV. My uncle wanted me to come live with him and his wife, but they argue and fight all the time. I definitely don't need that kind of drama in my life.

Alyssa raises her hand. "Who is Miss Lucy?" she questions when I focus my attention on her.

"You're not in school," Divine tells her with a chuckle. "You don't have to raise your hand."

"Whatever . . . ," Alyssa retorts.

"She's this lady I met when I was living on the streets," I explain. "Miss Lucy kinda became my foster mom. She made sure that I was safe. Some men attacked her when she first started living on the streets, so she looks out for girls like me."

"She was raped?" Divine asks, horrified.

I nod. "Since then, Miss Lucy keeps a bat with her at all times and some pepper spray. Even now that we're in the apartment, she has her bat under the bed, and she bought me one to keep in the sofa bed with me."

"I keep a bat under my bed, too," Alyssa says, nodding. "So does my mom. It's a girl's best friend."

Divine rubs sunscreen on her arms and legs. "I have one, too. I didn't until I moved in with Aunt Phoebe and Uncle Reed. Alyssa's mom is always walking out of her room ready to swing. Don't let her hear a noise in the house. She's up and checking it out."

"I think I'd rather have a gun," Mimi says while eyeing her fingernails. "I don't have time to be trying to beat down a man. I can just shoot them—it's better on your manicure, too."

Divine laughs. "Okay, Mimi. No more *Law & Order* or *Stylista* for you." She glances in my direction and says, "Kylie, this girl here actually made up a batch of homemade pepper spray. I don't know about you all, but I'm glad she's my friend. I'd hate to have her as an enemy."

Surprised that they, too, thought of those things, I nod in agreement.

"We girls have to protect ourselves and look good at the same time," Mimi goes on. "That's why I don't get physical with people that get on my last nerve. I'm not afraid to fight, but your face gets all twisted and contorted—you look ugly. Divine, you know . . ."

We crack up laughing.

"Laugh . . . I don't care," Mimi mutters. "There won't be no ugly pictures of me floating around the Internet. Chick fights gone wild. Pepper-spray their behinds, shoot them, or Taser them—you still look cute and well, they look however."

Rhyann gives Mimi a tap on the arm. "Yeah, I think we might need to keep you away from all action movies, period."

"If they don't bother me, I won't bother them."

"I'm with you on that," Alyssa agrees.

"Kylie, what was it like?" Mimi inquires, moving on to another subject. "Being homeless."

"Mimi, don't be rude," Rhyann cries, a frown on her face.

"Like you all don't want to know," she responds with no shame. "Kylie, does it bother you to talk about it? They won't say anything, but we might as well get it out in the open. That way it's done."

"It's fine," I say. "I don't mind talking about being homeless. My mom moved us out here, and things didn't go as planned. I ended up on the streets, but I was determined to make it. I tried to get a job, but I didn't have a phone, a car, or an address. My first night out, I met some other kids who were in the same situation, and I stayed with them. They wanted to do things like prostitute for money and some were drug users, so I left. I didn't want that to become my life. I'd heard about Safe Harbor Mission from one of them, so I headed downtown."

"Is that when you met Miss Lucy?" Divine asks.

I nod. "This guy tried to force me to go somewhere with him, but Miss Lucy ran him off with her bat. She promised to keep me safe and kind of showed me the ropes of homelessness. She kept telling me that I would survive this, and I did." I give a sad shake of my head. "Being homeless is no joke, though."

"Kylie, what was the hardest part for you?" Alyssa questions.

The answer to that was easy. "It was the lack of regard or even acknowledgment that I used to receive from people passing by. Some were so rude, and others pretended I didn't exist. Grandma Ellen always told me to say hello whenever I passed anyone. I used to see this one woman almost every day at the bus stop whenever I came to the shop. I was always saying good morning to her, but I never once received a response."

"I feel so bad that you had to go through that, Kylie. That's so totally wrong."

"Mimi, you don't have to feel sorry for me. I'm fine, and it was a valuable life experience for me. Besides, I never would've met Miss Lucy."

"Now that you have your apartment, are you going to go back to school?" Divine asks.

I shrug. "I don't know. I need to work and make some money—put a lil' something aside for that rainy day. I don't ever want to be this broke again."

Divine's eyes are full of wonder. "Kylie, I'm so glad we met you," she says. "Just looking at you, I never would've known that you were homeless."

"It was a bad time for me," I reply. "But my Grandma Ellen always said that God didn't promise us rainbows and daisies every day. She used to say that there was a reason for everything that happened, even though we might not understand why."

"Well, we're here, so we're going to have fun every day. Pretty soon you won't be thinking back on those days," Divine assures me. "You're one of us now, Kylie."

I frame a smile with my lips.

Deep down I know that I will never truly be one of them—these beautiful girls with parents who love them, who live in real homes with their families. I am grateful to have Miss Lucy and Miss Marilee in my life. They are as close to me as any family member, but they aren't my flesh-and-blood relatives.

"So how are you and T.J.?" Rhyann asks Divine, changing the subject.

"We're fine," she responds. "Like I told you, we have fun together, but we're not rushing into anything serious."

"Is that your boyfriend?" I inquire.

"Sort of," Divine replies.

"Divine, you need to tell the truth," Alyssa tells her. "You know that T.J. is your boo."

"Do all of you have boyfriends?" I ask out of curiosity. I've never really had a boyfriend, and right now, I'm not so sure that I even want one.

"I do," Alyssa states. "His name is Stephen, and he's gorgeous and sweet. We've been together since ninth grade."

Mimi finishes off her bottled water. "My boo's name is Kyle. His father is Ryan Marshall, the tennis pro."

"Cool," I say, not at all surprised that she'd be dating a celebrity's kid.

Rhyann says, "Traven is my sweetheart. We have been friends forever, but we just started dating."

They all look over at me. "I'm not involved with anyone,"

I say with a shrug. "Having a boyfriend isn't high on my list of priorities."

"Okay, Kylie sounds like Rhyann all last year," Mimi states with a chuckle. "She was singing that song up until prom."

Rhyann sips her soda. "I meant every word of it, too. Traven knows the deal. It's all about the education, baby."

I totally agree with Rhyann. When I think about my mama and the way her life turned out, I don't want anything close to that.

A couple of boys come over to where we're sitting.

They sit down and begin a conversation with us. It's pretty obvious to me that they want us to share our lunch with them.

Divine and Rhyann are polite but inform them that we're having a girl's day out and that we all have boyfriends. They get the hint and get up to leave as quickly as they came.

"That one in the red shorts didn't look like he'd hit a lick with a snake," I say.

They all turned to look at me.

"What did you just say?" they ask in unison.

"It means that one dude probably hasn't had a job for a while. He kept talking about all the stuff he was fixing to do. That's a whole lot of fixing and most of doing nothing, as my grandma used to say."

"He sure was staring at our fried chicken," Mimi interjected. "I think I even heard his stomach growl. Maybe they were hungry."

"I thought so, too," I say, feeling bad. I know what it feels like to be hungry, so I wish there was something I could do for them.

"I wouldn't have minded sharing," Divine puts in. "But we only brought enough food for us."

Rhyann glances over her shoulder, then back at us. "Don't worry too much about them. They're fine. That one guy just pulled out a beer from his bag. If he can drink beer, he can find himself some food. You're not even supposed to have beer on the beach."

Mimi's mother packed a lot of food for us, but I notice that I am the only one who eats my whole sub. Divine and the others barely finish off half of theirs. I notice Mimi looking at my empty plate, but she does not say anything.

When we finish eating, the girls and I run to the ocean, splashing water on one another. It feels so good just to be a sixteen-year-old for once. I don't have to worry about bills, rent, or anything. I can just enjoy being a teenager.

I'm having a pretty good time, but I can't help but wonder what they really think of me. Every now and then I catch Mimi staring at me. She's been nice and all, but I don't think she and I are going to be real close.

I don't get back home until shortly after six. The girls come upstairs with me to meet Miss Lucy, who has a fresh batch of chocolate peanut butter cookies ready and waiting for us.

"This is where you live," Mimi mutters.

"Yeah," I say. "What of it?"

She meets my gaze, then responds, "It's just that it seems a little on the small side for two people."

I cross my arms over my chest. "Miss Lucy and I are fine with our apartment."

"I think your place is nice," Alyssa interjects.

For a brief moment I'm not real sure I like Mimi. I don't need anyone in my life who thinks they are better than me.

The tense moment passes as we settle down to watch a movie and enjoy our cookies.

When it's almost nine o'clock, Mimi announces that she's tired and is ready to head home. Although they don't seem ready to leave, Divine and Alyssa have no choice but to leave, since they rode with her. Rhyann's brother is coming to pick her up from my apartment.

"Mimi has a habit of saying exactly what she thinks," Rhyann tells me after the others leave. "You just have to ignore her."

"I don't think she and I are gonna be best friends or any-thing," I say. "I can see that now."

"She'll come around," Rhyann assures me.

I shrug in nonchalance. "For the most part, I had a good time today. I'm glad y'all invited me to come along."

Rhyann is pleased to hear that. "Kylie, you're one of us. We're going to be doing a lot of things together this sum-mer."

I smile politely. I really like Rhyann and can relate most

to her because she doesn't come with a huge trust fund attached to her name. Divine is nice, and so is Alyssa, but Rhyann and I have so much more in common.

Rhyann looks out the window, then says, "My brother just pulled up. I'll see you on Tuesday at work."

I walk her downstairs.

"Thanks again for today," I tell her. "I had fun."

She hugs me. "Give me a call later if you're not busy."

When I go back upstairs, Miss Lucy says, "I don't think I've ever seen you this happy."

"Today was great," I say. "I had the best time with them. Divine and Alyssa are very cool. I'm not so sure about Mimi, though. She's a bit of a snob, but Rhyann, you know, is my girl."

"I love seeing you acting like a teenager," she tells me. "This is as it should be."

I couldn't agree more. Some kids might think it's pretty cool to be on your own, but it's not. It's hard work and pretty lonely.

The only thing that still bothers me is the way Mimi kept eyeing me when she thought I wasn't looking, plus her attitude about my home. Regardless of what Rhyann says, Mimi and I won't ever be B.F.F.'s. That's for sure.

Chapter 8

I'm surprised when Mimi comes up to me on Tuesday and says, "I'm having a slumber party this weekend at my house. Do you think you can come?"

I never expected her to invite me anywhere near her mansion, especially since she seems so stuck up. "Sure," I respond.

"Oh yeah, I have an appointment with Miss Marilee for a wash and set."

I quickly check her in.

Rhyann joins us a few minutes later. "I was just trying to reach you," she tells Mimi. "It went straight to voice mail."

Mimi checks her phone. "It's not turned on. I must have turned it off somehow." She gets upset at the thought. "There's no telling how many calls I've missed."

While she's checking her voice mail, Rhyann says to me, "Are you going to the slumber party?"

"I plan to," I respond.

"My brother will drop us off, so don't worry about a ride."

"Thanks, Rhyann."

Mimi puts her phone away. "So are we cool about Friday night? Slumber party at my house. Bring your cute pajamas and your favorite nail polish."

Rhyann escorts her to the shampoo area.

Cute pajamas? I sleep in a T-shirt and basketball shorts. I don't have any cute pajamas. I don't have any nail polish, either.

"What's with the frown?" Miss Marilee asks me.

"I don't know why I'm trying to hang with Mimi and Divine," I say in a low voice. "I don't have money or designer clothes, pajamas . . . stuff like that. Mimi just invited me to her house this weekend, and she said to bring nail polish and a pair of cute pajamas."

Miss Marilee smiles. "Hon, don't let this stress you out. If you need nail polish, you go next door and pick out a color.

We have some coupons for a free bottle. As for pajamas, Target has a sale on sleepwear this week."

"Really?"

She nods. "Kylie, you don't have to dress a certain way to be friends with Mimi and Divine. Just be yourself, hon."

Rhyann and I get our stuff out of her brother's car.

"I've never seen a house this huge before," I whisper to Rhyann. "How many bedrooms does this place have?"

"I think around eight," Rhyann answers.

I shake my head in disbelief as we walk up the circular driveway. Mimi runs out of the house to meet us.

"What took you two so long?" she asks.

"We had to wait on Brady to get off work," Rhyann responds. "Are Divine and Alyssa already here?"

Mimi nods. "They got here not too long ago."

We follow her into the house.

Mimi's bedroom is the size of my apartment. Now I understand why she was so shocked at my place.

Her mother has lunch already prepared, so we head down to the kitchen after putting our stuff away. I've never seen such a beautiful room for cooking. It looks like the ones I've seen in the magazines.

Mimi's brother comes down to the kitchen.

"Everybody, this is Chandler," Mimi says.

He's so cute that I find it hard not to stare. He picks a plate, piles it with a turkey sandwich, fruit, and chips, then comes to sit down beside me, which really makes me nervous.

"Chandler, what are you doing over here?" Mimi wants to know, wearing a look of irritation. "I already told you that my girls were going to be here this weekend. I thought you were going to kick it with your boy, Frankie."

"I'm just eating," he responds. "Frankie had to go out of town this weekend. His grandmother passed away."

"Can't you eat somewhere else?" she asks him pointedly.

Chandler eyes his sister hard. "I could, but I'm not going to," is his firm response.

Concentrating on my sandwich, I try to pretend that I don't notice him eyeballing me.

Rhyann apparently notices him watching me as well, because she keeps sending me secret smiles whenever I look at her.

"How do you like California?" Divine asks Chandler.

"It's okay," he responds. "I miss my friends back home, though."

"You should see all the girls at school," Mimi informs us. "They are all over him. I have no idea why."

Chandler sends Mimi a sharp look, which makes her laugh.

He glances over at me, but I keep my head down, praying he won't ask me anything about school.

When Chandler is finished eating, he excuses himself and leaves.

"Mimi, your brother is too cute," Alyssa tells her.

"He sure is," Rhyann says in agreement. "I think he's interested in Kylie, too."

"No, he's not," Mimi retorts quickly. "I don't know where you came up with that, but it's totally not true."

Heat rises up to my cheeks. "That's fine with me," I respond without looking up. I guess Mimi thinks that her brother is too good for a girl like me. I'm fine to hang around with, but not good enough to date her brother.

Whatever.

After lunch, we go back up to Mimi's room to change into swimsuits. This time they are all wearing different ones than the ones they wore to the beach. I slip on the only one that I own.

Mimi notices and says, "Would you like to wear one of my swimsuits, Kylie?"

I glance down at my body, then back up at her. "Why would I want to do that? The one I have on is clean, isn't it?"

"I just thought I'd offer," she responds.

"Do you have a problem with what I'm wearing?" I ask. Might as well mention the elephant in the room.

Mimi glances over at Divine before turning to me. "No, I just didn't want you to feel bad. We're all wearing different swimsuits."

I soften my voice, seeing her point. "It doesn't bother me, Mimi."

"Okay, then . . ." She walks toward the door. "I can't wait to get into the pool."

Rhyann walks beside me. "You sure you're okay, Kylie?"

"I'm fine," I reply.

I sit on the edge of the pool while everyone else splashes around in the water. Rhyann swims over to me and climbs out. She takes a seat beside me. "Why won't you get in?"

"I'm not in the mood for swimming right now," I say. "Especially so soon after lunch."

Rhyann doesn't buy that excuse, though. "Mimi doesn't mean any harm, Kylie. She's a bit of an airhead. She says what comes to mind without thinking, but we love her."

"I'm fine, really."

"C'mon and get in the pool with us," Divine calls out to me. "We're here to have a good time."

I jump into the pool but stay as far away from Mimi as possible. I'm not feeling her at all.

An hour later, we settle down in her bedroom.

"Chandler was watching you from his window," Rhyann whispers to me while Mimi is on her cell phone talking to her boyfriend. "Did you see him?"

"He might have been looking at you, Divine, or Alyssa," I respond.

"Nope, he was staring you down."

I glance over my shoulder at Mimi, and then back at Rhyann. "Don't say anything around Mimi. Okay? I don't need her going cold on me."

"She'll be fine," Rhyann says. "If Chandler likes you, then there's nothing she can do about it."

"He doesn't like me, Rhyann," I protest.

"Humph," she responds. "I know what I'm talking about, Kylie. That dude is definitely into you."

Her words make my stomach quiver in nervous energy. Chandler is cute and all, but just the thought that he might be interested in me . . . wow. I'm not real sure how I feel about it.

Mimi mellows out for the rest of the evening and we end up having a great time—that is, until Chandler makes an appearance. She quickly makes him leave when she catches him looking at me.

This time Divine notices it, too. "Meems, what's up with you?" she asks. "Why are you tripping on your brother like that?"

"It's our night and Chandler doesn't need to be in our business," she responds, pretending innocence. "This evening is all about us." Yet Mimi is watching me the whole time.

She and I both know that despite what she is saying, there is a whole lot more going on. The truth is that she doesn't want Chandler anywhere near me.

I'm an early riser. We didn't fall asleep until well after three in the morning, but I wake up shortly after 6:00 a.m.

Being as quiet as I can, I shower and get dressed. I ease out of the room and head downstairs to the kitchen. I'm surprised to find Chandler in there cooking.

"What are you doing up?" he asks me. "I figured you all would be sleeping until at least noon."

"I don't need as much sleep," I respond.

"I'm the same way," Chandler tells me as he flips a pancake. "I thought I'd make you ladies some breakfast."

"That's really sweet."

He glances over at me and says in mock seriousness, "Don't tell anybody. I don't want to ruin my rep."

I chuckle. "Do you need any help?"

"That depends," he responds. "Can you cook?"

"I've been cooking since I was nine years old."

"Okay," Chandler says, not convinced. "But can you cook?"

I hold up my hand like a Girl Scout. "Yeah, I can cook."

While he works on the pancakes, I make bacon and sausages. When we're done, Chandler says, "I don't think we should wait on the others to eat. We'll be starving if we do. Mimi will sleep until noon if nobody wakes her up."

"So what are you suggesting?" I ask, my arms folded across my chest.

"Let's have breakfast."

Chandler and I fix our plates and take seats at the glass table near the French doors leading out to the patio.

"So, Kylie, where are you from?" Chandler asks me after we say grace.

"North Carolina," I respond between bites.

"How are you liking it out here?"

I give a slight shrug. "It's okay, I guess. How about you? Do you really like living in California?"

Chandler nods. "I like spending time with my dad. He's always so busy, though." He steals a peek over his shoulder before saying, "I'm not sure about Dean—sometimes I feel like she doesn't really want me here."

"She seems pretty nice to me."

"That's because you don't live here. She doesn't really talk to me much, and only when my dad is around. She ignores me the rest of the time."

"Do you miss your mom?" I ask.

Chandler nods. "She sent me out here because I was tripping, you know. I was hanging with the wrong crowd and I wanted to be with my dad."

"Do you want to go back home?"

"Not really," he responds. "I like school and I do want to go to college out here, so I might as well stay around."

Before I can respond, Mimi storms into the kitchen, saying, "Well, isn't this cute? What are you two doing?"

Divine and Alyssa come in seconds later, followed by Rhyann.

"We're having breakfast," Chandler says dryly. "I thought you could've figured that much out, Mimi."

She looks furious.

"Y'all were sleeping, so I came down here to keep from waking you up," I explain. "Chandler was in here fixing breakfast, so I offered to help with the cooking."

"I bet you did," Mimi utters.

"What's that supposed to mean?" I ask, offended.

"You couldn't wait to be alone with my brother."

I push away from the table and rise to my feet. "Mimi, he was making breakfast for us, so I thought I'd show my appreciation by helping out. I don't know what your problem is, but I'm not going to stay here another minute. I'm out of here."

"Kylie, don't leave," Divine interjects. "Mimi, maybe you need to go back to bed or something, because you really are in a foul mood."

"Chandler, you need to stay away from my friends," Mimi tells him.

"Why don't you say what you really mean?" I say. "Chandler, she wants you to stay away from me because I used to be homeless."

Rhyann eyed Mimi. "Tell Kylie that she's wrong."

The room is thick with a tense silence.

"I'm going to get my things and I'm out," I say, heading toward the stairs.

Divine follows me.

"Kylie, I'm so sorry," she tells me as we head up the stairs. "I don't know what's wrong with Mimi."

"It's fine," I say, fighting back tears. "I just want to go home."

Chandler comes into the room and says, "I'll drive you."

I shake my head. "You don't have to do that."

"I want to," he counters, pretty annoyed himself. "I'm driving you home, Kylie. Right now I need to get out of here myself."

As much as I don't want to admit it, Mimi's treatment of me really hurts. I pack up my backpack and rush downstairs.

Alyssa is standing near the front door. "Kylie, I'm sorry."

"It's not your fault," I respond. "I hope to see you again, Alyssa."

"You will," Divine says from behind me. "We're still friends, and we're going to hang out this summer."

Rhyann rushes over to me. "I'll give you a call later. Girlfriend is seriously tripping this morning."

Chandler and I walk outside to his car, a nice-looking Ford Mustang. Mimi drives a BMW convertible. "I don't like foreign cars," he tells me, as if sensing my thoughts. "I've always wanted a Mustang."

"It's very nice," I say as I get in. "It still smells brand-new."

He laughs. "I've had it for a week."

"Chandler, I really appreciate you taking me home."

"Hey, I'm sorry about my sister. She's tripping."

I agree. "All we were doing is talking."

A look passes over his face that I can't read. "Kylie, I like you and I don't care what my sister thinks—I want to be your friend."

I can sense trouble brewing, and I point out, "Chandler, I'm not trying to come between family. Mimi is your sister."

"You don't have to worry about that," he scoffs. "I can handle Mimi. She can't tell me who I can talk to or spend time with."

I glance over at him and ask, "Why do you want to be my friend? You did hear what I said, didn't you? I used to be homeless. I work at the hair salon where Mimi gets her hair done."

"And?" Chandler responds.

"That doesn't bother you?"

"Why should it?" Chandler turns and rests his hand on my headrest. "I'm not like my sister, Kylie. I grew up in a regular neighborhood and I went to public school until moving out here. My mom is a nurse and she works a full-time job. The money my dad sends is put into a trust for me and my college fund."

I smile, touched that he would let me know. "So what you're trying to say is that our lives are not that different."

Chandler nods.

"That's where you're wrong," I tell him, waving at the magnificent house. "Our lives are very different, Chandler. More than you could ever imagine."

Chapter 9

"I can't believe that girl would behave that way," Miss Lucy comments.

"She did," I say. "Mimi acted like I was nothing but trash. Her brother wanted our number, though, so I gave it to him. I like Chandler."

The telephone rings.

I answer it. "Hello."

"Kylie, it's Divine. I wanted to make sure you made it

home okay, and to apologize for Mimi's attitude. We left right after you did, because she was wrong."

"I don't want to cause any friction between y'all," I tell Divine. "I don't have to be a part of your circle."

"You're not getting off that easy. We've decided you're one of us, Kylie. Mimi just has to stop tripping, and we told her so."

I feel like I'm causing a rift between the girls and Mimi, and that's not what I set out to do. They have been friends a long time. "Divine, don't worry about me. You and Mimi go way back. You haven't known me very long."

"It's not about how long I've known you, Kylie. Mimi came off wrong with you and she needed to know it. Being friends is about being honest with each other."

We talk for another twenty minutes. Before we hang up, Divine invites me over to her house to spend time with her and Alyssa.

"I'd like that," I tell her. She really is nice.

"Cool. My mom is going to send a car for you."

"That sounds deluxe."

Divine laughs. "It's just a car, Kylie. It beats public transportation any day, in my opinion. I'm not knocking the bus or anything," she adds, "but car service is just the best, next to riding around in a limo."

"I wouldn't know," I say, laughing.

"I'll see you tomorrow."

I hang up the phone and announce, "Divine invited me over tomorrow after church."

"I heard," Miss Lucy responds. "I think it's wonderful."

The telephone rings again and I answer. This time it is Rhyann.

"I'm fine," I tell her.

"I'm not," she says. "I'm so pissed at Mimi. How could she treat you like that?"

"She's your friend," I remind her.

"Mimi won't be, if she keeps this mess up," Rhyann says. "She was wrong, and I'm not going to let her get away with it. Now I know how she really feels about me."

I don't believe that. "I think it's just me," I tell Rhyann.

"Nope. I'm sure if Chandler had shown any interest in me, she'd feel the same way. I'm disappointed in Mimi, because I thought she was different. I knew she was a little snobby by the things she said, but . . .

"Anyway, enough about Meems. Did Chandler get your phone number?"

A grin spreads across my face. "Yeah."

"I knew it," Rhyann shouts, forcing me to move the receiver from my ear. "I knew that Chandler was into you."

"We're just trying to be friends. That's all."

"Friendship is a good place to start, Kylie."

Chandler and I spend two hours on the phone talking. A couple of times, Mimi enters his bedroom, trying to talk to him, but he always makes her leave.

I'm mildly surprised when Chandler tells me that he

wants to take me to the movies one night next week. I promise to get back to him with an answer.

He seems really nice, and he feels almost the same way about his dad that I feel about my mom. Chandler resents his father for never spending time with him although he constantly promises to do better by him. Even now that Chandler's here in California and in the same house with his father, he hardly sees him. His dad leaves early in the morning for the studio and doesn't get home until late in the night. When he's not at the studio, he's traveling somewhere to do a movie.

"Chandler, I'm sure your father loves you," I tell him. "He may work a lot, but your dad is making sure you have everything you need."

"I don't want all of this stuff," he retorts. "Kylie, I want time with my dad. That's all."

I totally understand. I want my mama to spend time with me and forget about a man just for once.

After I hang up with Chandler, I settle down to watch some television with Miss Lucy.

"Have you talked with Mimi?" she asks me.

"No, ma'am. She kept trying to interrupt Chandler while he was on the phone with me. He told me that he finally locked her out of the room." I glance over at Miss Lucy. "Mimi and I aren't gonna be friends. I see that now."

"It's her loss, then."

I smile. "Yeah, it sure is."

My thoughts travel to Chandler, who is nothing like his sister. I like talking to him, but I'm pretty sure his family will put pressure on him to leave me alone. I silently vow to keep from getting involved with him so that I don't end up hurt.

I'm also determined not to get too wrapped up in a boy. I need to focus on my future if I want to make something out of myself. I'm definitely going to prove to Mimi that I'm just as good as she is, even though I don't have her family's money.

I have a heart and I don't judge people by their circumstances, so I'm already one up on her.

Mimi comes to the shop the next day. She and Rhyann talk outside for a few minutes. I'm fairly sure they're discussing me, but I don't care. I'm done with Mimi.

Rhyann comes back inside and says, "Do you want to have lunch with me and Mimi?"

I shake my head. "I brought some egg salad from home, so I'll eat here. But thanks for asking."

Rhyann studies my face. "It was Mimi's idea, Kylie."

"The answer is still no. Rhyann, please don't try to force a friendship between me and Mimi. It's just not going to happen."

"She came here to apologize."

I look out the window. "Really? Is that why she barely said two words to me?"

"Mimi feels bad about what happened."

I shrug in nonchalance. "She doesn't have to feel bad about anything. She's stuck up and she looks down on others. That's just who she is. Rhyann, go have lunch with your friend. I'm okay. This isn't gonna affect my relationship with you. At least, I hope it doesn't."

"Girl, pleez . . . ," Rhyann mutters. "Our friendship has nothing to do with Mimi."

She leaves.

Although I would never mention this to Rhyann, I feel conflicted. A part of me wishes she had chosen to stay mad at Mimi just a little while longer so she could feel what I feel—like an outsider.

Chandler wants to see me later tonight, but I'm not ready for that. Besides, it still bothers me that Mimi has a problem with me talking to her brother.

I'm in the break room eating my lunch when Rhyann returns forty-five minutes later. Mimi walks in with her.

"Kylie, I came here to talk to you, but . . . ," Mimi says. "Well, you looked like you didn't want to be bothered."

I wipe my mouth on the corner of my paper napkin. "Talk about what?"

"I think we need to clear the air about what happened at my house."

"Oh, I think we're pretty clear."

Mimi sits down in the empty chair beside me. "I like you, Kylie. I think you're a really nice person."

"So, why do you have a problem with your brother talking to me?" I ask. "It's not like we're involved. We just *talk*."

"I'm sorry for the way I acted. Chandler isn't from here, and I guess I was just being overprotective."

I look her straight in the eye. "Are you really sorry?"

Mimi meets my gaze. "Yes, I am, Kylie. Even though I haven't been acting like it, I do want us to be friends."

"You have a weird way of showing it."

Mimi glances over at Rhyann and says, "I guess I deserve that."

"You were wrong," Rhyann tells her.

"I hope that we can start over," Mimi says to me.

I think about that and nod. I really don't want to cause problems between these old friends. "I'd like that."

She holds out her hand to me. "Friends?"

I shake her hand. "Friends."

Mimi releases a sigh of relief. "Whew! I'm so glad this is over. Why don't we go out to dinner this evening to celebrate?"

"I guess I can do it," I say. Dinner tonight is probably going to set me back until my next payday, but I don't tell Rhyann or Mimi.

Everything will be okay, I tell myself. Tonight is a special occasion.

Chapter 10

Chandler surprises me at the salon the next day, wanting to take me to lunch.

Rhyann urges me to go with him. Deep down, I really want to spend time with him, so I accept his invitation.

"I'm glad you said yes," he tells me when we walk across the street to the deli. "We talk on the phone almost every night, but you always turn me down when I ask you on a date."

"This is a date?" I ask, my stomach doing a little flip.

He meets my gaze. "I'd like it to be, Kylie. Look, I'm very interested in you, and I know you like me, too. You don't have to worry about Mimi. This is about you and me. She'll get over herself."

"I just don't want to come between you and your sister."

"You won't," Chandler assures me.

"Chandler, I can't help but wonder why me," I say after we get our food and sit at one of the tables outside.

"You're beautiful and intelligent," he says simply. "I know life has been a little crazy for you, but you are a survivor. You haven't given up, and if you really want to know the truth, I admire you."

His words render me speechless. I feel like a complete fraud right now.

Chandler scans my face. "Kylie, what's wrong?"

"Your words just took me by surprise," I say. "Chandler, I'm not perfect or anything. I'm just trying to get to the point where I can take care of myself. I want to go back to school in the fall and I don't know what to expect, but I have to make it work."

He smiles at me. "You will." He reaches over and takes me by the hand. "You can trust me, Kylie."

This is the best lunch I have ever had. A part of me does not want to go back to the shop, but I still need a paycheck.

I stop at Chandler's car on the way back, and we talk for a few more minutes before I have to go inside.

Chandler gives me a hug and a polite kiss on the cheek. He gets in his car, and I wave as he drives away.

Yet my happy smile vanishes when I come face-to-face with my mama.

"Mama, what are you doing here?" I ask, trying to keep the panic from my voice. She's wearing a dress that's so tight, she can't possibly have on a pair of panties beneath. I frown. *"What do you have on?"*

Mama ignores my questions and looks me up and down. "So who was that?"

"Who?" I ask, stalling for time. I pray Rhyann or Miss Marilee doesn't walk outside the shop.

"That boy that was all over you."

"He wasn't all over me, and he is just a friend."

She flashes a sly smile. "I saw y'all sitting over there having lunch. Where did you meet him?"

"Mama, he is just a friend. I have to go."

"Why? You can't spend a few minutes with your mama? You haven't seen me in a while, but I guess you don't miss me."

"I have a job and I need to get back to work so I don't lose it," I tell her.

She peeks inside the salon. "I guess you work here in this fancy beauty shop."

I don't want to talk about that. Instead I repeat my question. "What are you doing here?"

With her hands on her hips, she responds, "Since I was driving by and saw you, and since I don't ever hear from you, I figured I'd stop to see how you doing. Kylie, you may have moved out of the house, but I'm still your mama."

"Nice of you to remember that," I say tightly. "It's a little too late, as far as I'm concerned." I steal a peek over my shoulder to see if anyone from the salon can see us. I desperately hope not. I don't want anybody to know that this woman dressed like a hoochie is my mama.

"Kylie, so how much money you making here in this place?" she demands.

"Not a lot," I answer honestly.

Mama screws her face into a frown. "Then why on earth are you working here? I thought I taught you better than that. Please tell me that you at least getting tips?"

I don't respond. I just want her to go away. *Far away.*

"Did you hear me?"

"I know what you want and you might as well forget about it," I say. "I don't have any money, Mama."

"When do you get paid, then?"

"I don't know," I lie. "Maybe it's Friday. I forgot to ask. I was just happy about getting the job." I move to walk around my mother. "Mama, I really have to get back to work so that I don't lose my job."

She grabs my arm just as I step past her. "Hey, where are you living?"

"In a shelter, Mama," I answer. "Where are you living? Did you get evicted?"

"Clyde and I still live in the apartment," she responds. "You should come by sometime so that he can meet you. You know, he might end up being your daddy. He really loves me to death."

"I don't think so, Mama," I say. "I don't need a daddy."

I can tell she doesn't like the tone of my voice. "I'm grown, and if I want to get married, I will."

"Getting married would be a change for you," I respond.

"Clyde is a nice guy, Kylie. You shouldn't judge him before you meet him."

"Does he have a job?" I ask pointedly.

"He's self-employed," my mama responds.

"I hope it's legal."

She blinks at that remark and takes a few moments to collect herself. I know I've guessed right. "Hey, do they still need any help in the salon?" she asks me. "Maybe I could do some braiding. You don't need a license to braid hair."

"They already have two people braiding hair," I respond quickly. "They don't need any more help."

The last thing I want is to have my mama working with me. I am not about to let her embarrass me up in there. She is too lazy to work, anyway—I don't know who she is trying to fool.

"I have to go, Mama." I try to walk around her, but she's not giving up.

"Kylie, I know how you are about money. I just need a few dollars. I can give it back to you tomorrow. Clyde's picking up his payment tomorrow."

My arms folded across my chest, I ask, "What exactly does he do?"

"What does it matter?" she responds. "The man makes a living, and he gets paid a lot of money. We're already looking at houses. Kylie, we're gonna be a family."

I'm outraged that she would think that way. "Mama, why weren't we a family before? How does having Clyde in your life make us a family?"

When she does not respond, I say wearily, "I really need to get inside, Mama. Oh, and please do me a favor. Don't come up to my job anymore."

"You still haven't told Marilee the truth?" Miss Lucy asks after I tell her about seeing my mother outside the salon earlier.

"No, ma'am," I admit. "Miss Lucy, it's because I don't want her to think badly of me. I know that she had to see me standing outside the shop talking to her. Do you think she's gonna ask me about my mama? Like who she is and how I know her?"

Miss Lucy shrugs. "She might, and then again, she might not. I don't know for sure, but I do think that if you're so worried about it, you need to sit Marilee down and tell her the truth."

There is a knock on the door, startling both of us.

Miss Lucy looks at me. "Are you expecting someone, Kylie?"

I shake my head.

"Bring me your bat," she whispers.

Yet we won't be needing any bats. I sigh in frustration when I hear my mama's voice whining, "C'mon, Kylie, open up."

I walk to the door, opening it. I gasp in surprise at the sight of a man standing beside my mother. This has to be Clyde. He is the same man I saw her with that day at the shops.

"How did you find this place?" I ask. "What are you doing here?"

I cannot believe she actually came back up to my job and followed me home like a spy. Mama brushes past me, along with Clyde, her current flavor of the month.

Mama glances around the apartment. "Kylie, I thought you said that you been living in a shelter. Why you lying to me and trying to be all secretive?"

She eyes Miss Lucy up and down and asks, "Is this your place?"

"I don't know you, and I don't owe you any answers."

I notice the way Miss Lucy is inching over to the sofa. She'll pull that bat out in a flash if she deems it necessary.

"This is my mama, Serena," I say to Miss Lucy. "Mama, this is Miss Lucy."

Mama introduces Clyde, then says, "If my child is living here, you'd better tell me something. Somebody gonna tell me something. *I mean that.*"

"Mama, leave her alone," I interject. "Miss Lucy is kind enough to let me stay here with her, and I won't let you harass her."

"Why you being all charitable to my daughter? What do you want from her?"

I can tell Miss Lucy is trying hard not to cuss my mama flat out. "She don't want nothing from me," I say. "She's just letting me stay here until I can afford to get my own place."

"This is nice," Mama says to Clyde. "It's on the small side, though."

"It has a roof and doors," I respond. "I appreciate it, and I'm happy here." I start walking toward the door. "You've seen where I live, so now you and Clyde can go be happy in your apartment."

"What you doing about school?"

As if she really cares.

"I don't go to school."

Mama folds her arms across her chest. "Oh, so you gonna be a sixteen-year-old dropout now?"

"I'm planning to go back to school in the fall or find an alternative school Miss Marilee was telling me about."

Frowning, Mama questions, "Who is that?"

"She's the lady I work for."

"If you gonna be doing all that, you might as well come back home with us so that you can help your mama out," she says firmly. "I gave you life and you owe me that much."

Miss Lucy is bristling, but she holds her tongue. I know she's trying not to lose her religion.

"Mama, I'm not going anywhere," I reply. "I like living here with Miss Lucy. I really don't want to live with you and your boyfriend. Been there, done that."

"Now that you got a lil' job, you think you better than us, huh." She walks over to Clyde and says, "Can you believe this mess? You see how she treats me?"

"I don't think I'm better or anything," I say. "I just want to live without worrying about an eviction notice. I don't want to worry about the lights being off because you'd rather go shopping than pay the electric bill." My chest is getting tight, but I force myself to continue.

"Mama, I'm tired of moving from place to place. You've ruined your credit and mine. I've had more stuff in my name, but none of it was for me."

My mama draws back her hand to hit me, but Miss Lucy springs into action, stepping between me and the woman who gave me life. "There will be none of that in this place. Serena, you've said your piece, but it's long past time for you and Clyde to leave."

"I'm not leaving without my child," Mama tells her nastily. "She belongs at home with me."

"Do you really want us to call the police?" I warn her. "I don't know if Clyde has any legal issues, but I do know you got some outstanding warrants. You'll end up in jail, and I'll have to go into foster care. Miss Lucy will apply to be my foster mother and I'll only end up back here anyway."

I can tell from the expression on my mama's face that she is furious. "You need to stop telling all my business."

I meet my mama's gaze straight on. "Maybe if you stopped breaking the law and pay your bills, then I wouldn't have anything to tell, would I? I don't want to be mean or disrespectful, but you won't leave me alone."

Clyde heads toward the door. "C'mon, baby. If she don't want to come with us, let her stay on here. You don't need all this drama."

Mama looks like she isn't going anywhere.

"Kylie will be fine," Miss Lucy tells her. "You know where she is, and she isn't going anywhere."

"She's my daughter," Mama shouts. "Just so we clear on everything."

"Then you need to start acting like her mama," Miss Lucy retorts.

"I'm grown," my mama responds. "I can do what I want to do. Kylie is a child. She has no right trying to dictate my life."

Clyde takes her by the hand and leads her to the door. "Let's get out of here."

I run into Miss Lucy's arms as soon as they leave. "I don't want to go home with her," I say. "Miss Lucy, we've got to find a way for me to stay here with you."

"I didn't like the way that man was eyeing you," Miss Lucy tells me. "He was looking a little too hard at you. Don't worry, Kylie, we're gonna find a way to make this work out."

Chapter 11

Last night was a bad night for me. I didn't sleep well at all because of that visit from my mama and Clyde. I can't help but take their showing up the way they did as a bad sign. Now that they know where I live, I won't ever be able to escape them.

I steal a peek at the clock on the table and nearly freak out.

I overslept and am going to be late for work if I don't get a move on.

"Kylie, you awake?" I hear Miss Lucy ask from across the room. "You need to get up, don't you?"

I swing my legs to the edge of the sofa bed. "I'm up."

I run to the bathroom, take a shower, brush my teeth, and comb my hair back into a ponytail.

"You tossed and turned all night long," Miss Lucy tells me when I come out wearing my robe.

"I didn't sleep too well." Fast as lightning, I slip on my black pants and shirt. I'm so glad I ironed them last night. "I kept thinking about Clyde and my mama."

"They can't hurt you," Miss Lucy assures me. "They can't even get into this apartment without you inviting them inside. You just keep that in mind."

I nod, but inside I'm scared. She doesn't know how my mama can get.

"Don't forget your lunch," she reminds me. Miss Lucy makes a lunch for me almost every night and places it in the refrigerator. Most of the staff at Crowning Glory bring their lunch because eating out all the time can get expensive.

"I won't," I respond, grabbing the bag from the fridge, then picking up my backpack. "I need to get out of here so I can make my bus. I'll see you this evening."

I send up a prayer of thanks when I run into Lisa at the elevators.

"Hey, Kylie, you want to ride with me to work? I have an early client this morning—and one tomorrow, if you're interested."

"Thank you so much. I'm running so late."

She surveys my face. "You okay?"

I nod. "I just didn't sleep well."

When we arrive at work, Miss Marilee greets us with a smile. "Hello, ladies."

"Morning, Miss Marilee," I say in response.

After I have everything prepared, I navigate to the break room to make myself a cup of hot tea to calm my still frazzled nerves.

Not only does my mama know where I live but she also knows where I work. How long before she comes into the salon to start trouble?

Rhyann doesn't come in until noon, so I don't really have anyone to talk to. I keep my eyes glued to the door just in case my mama decides to bust up in here. I pray that she won't, but with her, you never know what she'll do.

I've got to find a way to tell Miss Marilee the truth. I don't want her finding out any other way. I toy with the idea of telling her later today. I'm working until five, and she's leaving around that time because she has to teach Bible study at her church at six.

Out of the blue, Mimi comes in with Chandler.

"Kylie, hey, girl," she greets me. "Chandler wants dreadlocks, so he's here to see Marsha."

I smile. "I'll check you in."

While I'm checking him in on the computer, he smiles back.

"You're checked in," I say as calmly and professionally as I can manage. "Your stylist will be with you shortly."

"Thank you, Kylie. It's good to see you."

"You, too."

Mimi's mouth tightens as she stands there beside Chandler, tapping her foot impatiently.

He looks over at her and asks, "What's up with you?"

"You need to come on," Mimi snaps. "We don't have all day."

"You go on," Chandler tells her. "You need a whole lot more work done than I do."

Mimi rolls her eyes at him before stomping off.

"She really doesn't like you talking to me," I whisper to Chandler. "I told you, I'm not gonna come between you and your sister."

He dismisses my words with a wave of his hand. "You're not," he replies. "I'm not going to let Mimi dictate who I'm friends with or who I date. You shouldn't, either. I think her boyfriend is a joke, but she doesn't want to hear it. She's quick to tell me to mind my own business."

I shift uncomfortably in my chair because I can feel the heat of his gaze on me. Finally, Marsha comes to take him to her station.

A few minutes later, Rhyann rushes up to the reception desk. "Looks like you and Chandler are really hitting it off."

"Mimi's not too happy about it," I respond gloomily.

"That's her problem."

"How do you feel about it?" I ask.

She waggles her hand. "Chandler's cool and all, but I do worry about him playing games with you. I don't want you to get hurt."

"I'm not really looking for a boyfriend," I tell her with a shrug. "Just some friends to hang out with, so you don't have anything to worry about."

She smiles, not believing me for a second. "I think Chandler's going to look cute with dreads, don't you think?"

I nod in agreement. "Your brother's look is really nice. I like Brady's hair a lot."

Rhyann made a face. "Please don't tell Brady that. He's so conceited."

We chuckle.

"Seriously, Rhyann," I say. "I'm really not looking for a relationship with Chandler or anyone. If it happens, it happens."

"Sounds good to me," Rhyann says.

Chandler comes over to me when Marsha's finished with him.

I break into a big grin. "Your hair looks good."

"I don't know," he responds, tilting his head back and forth. "I have all these little twists sticking out everywhere."

"Your hair looks nice."

Mimi joins us. "Kylie's right. You look nice, Chandler."

He places an arm around her. "So do you, Mimi. You working that weave."

"You don't have to tell everybody," she tells him and gives him a sharp jab in the arm.

Laughing, I ring up his list of services and give him the total.

He pays me for his services and Mimi's. *He's such a nice brother,* I think to myself.

"Hey, did you get a cell phone yet?" he asks me. I'd been telling him for the past couple of days that I was getting a prepaid one. I decided to break down and get one after Rhyann told me I was probably the only teen in Los Angeles without a cell phone.

"I'm getting one on Saturday."

"Don't forget to give me the number," he tells me.

"I won't."

Mimi pushes him toward the door. "C'mon, we need to get home. Mother wants me to clean out my closet, and I don't want to hear her nagging me about it. You can call Kylie later."

Once they leave, Rhyann walks up to the reception desk. "You know, I asked Mimi why she's acting that way."

I glance over at her. "What did she say?"

"Just that she and her brother are getting close and she doesn't want to share him with anyone right now."

"Do you believe her?"

Rhyann meets my gaze. "I guess I have to take her word for it. B.F.F.'s don't lie to each other."

Her words feel like a stab to my chest. I've been lying to

all of them about my mother. Any time now, and my lie will be exposed.

I take my lunch break at two o'clock. Rhyann has a lull in shampooing hair so she ventures into the break room to sit and talk with me. When a client comes into the salon, she has to hurry back to work.

I finish my lunch in solitude. Afterward, I head off to the bathroom to brush my teeth. Greeting customers with tuna salad breath is not cool.

My nerves prickle every time I glimpse a black Ford Explorer parked across the street. I check the door every now and then to see if I can spot her lurking outside somewhere, but I don't see her anywhere.

My work shift ends two hours later, and still no sight of Mama.

Humming softly, I pack up my stuff and leave the salon on my way to the bus stop. I'm so grateful that Mama had the good sense to stay away.

At least until I have a chance to explain everything to Miss Marilee. I would've talked to her after I got off, but she was with a client and would be with her for a while. She was putting in a weave, which China was going to have to finish, because Miss Marilee had to leave before she had time to complete it. I decide I'll just wait and talk to her tomorrow.

Miss Lucy is on me as soon as I get home. "Did you talk to Marilee?"

"No, ma'am," I answer. "I am gonna tell her, I promise."

"Honey, what are you so afraid of? Marilee isn't gonna turn on you. She's not like that, Kylie."

"You're right, Miss Lucy. I've already decided to tell her tomorrow. She had a lot going on today, but I will tell her as soon as I get to work."

Dinner is ready, so we sit down to eat and discuss our day. Miss Lucy is in some pain, so she called the doctor and is going to see him tomorrow. The woman across the hall is driving her.

"It's a bunch of nice folks here in this building," she tells me.

I agree.

When we finish eating, I offer to clean up to give Miss Lucy a break.

Chandler calls me shortly after eight.

"What are you up to?" he asks.

"I just finished cleaning up the kitchen," I say. "I was thinking about doing some reading before you called. You saved me from reading *Gone With the Wind* for the twentieth time."

"I just finished up some laundry," he says darkly. "I'm glad it's done. I hate washing clothes."

I smile. "You do laundry? I thought maybe you had the housekeeper do it or something."

"No, that's Mimi," he responds. "My mother started making me do my own laundry once I turned thirteen."

"I've been washing my own stuff since I was about twelve years old, I think."

He's not going to talk about that for long, and our conversation turns to our plans for the summer.

"I plan on enjoying these next few weeks," Chandler tells me. "I'm almost done with the summer course I had to take."

"Are you nervous about going to Stony Hills Prep?" I ask. "Rhyann loves it there."

"A little," he admits. "That's just because I don't know what to expect."

"I heard Mimi say that you're going to be playing football for the school."

"Yeah," Chandler confirms. "They have a pretty good team."

We talk about the beach, favorite foods, movies, and practically everything under the sun. Chandler and I laugh as we watch the same sitcom while chatting.

He changes the subject by asking, "Kylie, when can we go out on a real date?"

I chuckle. "Chandler, you're about as subtle as a man wearing a cross-your-heart bra."

His shout of laughter sounds like music to my ears. "So is that a yes?"

"Sure. I think I'd really like to get to know you a little better," I say. "And it's time you met Miss Lucy. She's my guardian."

"I don't have a problem with that."

"Great."

I can't stop smiling for the rest of the evening. Chandler and I are going on a real date. I still can't believe that this amazing guy is interested in me.

Another thought comes to my mind, though, and my smile disappears. What if he's just trying to get into my pants? Maybe all this is to trick the poor chick into sleeping with him. I glance down at the thin band on my left ring finger. It's my purity ring.

If Chandler's out for sex, then he's going to be disappointed, because I'm not about to go there with him or anyone else.

Chapter 12

"K"ylie, we're going to the Keyshia Cole concert," Rhyann announces while we are folding fresh towels. "Do you want to go? Dee's picking up tickets this afternoon."

"I can't," I respond. Deep down, I really want to go with them, but I can't afford to spend money for recreation. I want to make sure that Miss Lucy and I can get by in case she doesn't get her disability.

Miss Marilee has been helping her out with all of that,

but we don't know for sure if she'll be getting a check. Miss Lucy's had some problems getting all the information the VA needs from her.

"You sure you don't want to go?" Rhyann asks. "We're going to have a great time. We all ride together in a limo, have dinner first, and then go to the concert."

"I can't because I need to save my money."

She realizes that it's a problem. "I'll pay for you," she offers.

"Naw," I tell her. "Y'all have fun. Maybe I can go with you next time."

"Well, we're going to get together tonight for dinner. You coming with us for that, right?"

"Rhyann, I can't. Don't get me wrong—I'd love to go, but I need to save."

"Kylie, why don't you let me treat you?" she asks. "I don't mind. You're my girl and you need to have some fun sometimes."

I try to pass it off as no big deal. "I don't want you spending your hard-earned money on me. I hope there will be other times for me to join y'all."

I meant what I said about never being broke again. Living on the streets wasn't fun for me, and I intend to avoid it at all costs.

"I really do understand that you want to save money," Rhyann says. "Especially after everything you have been through."

"I'ma put some aside for recreation, as my Grandma Ellen used to say. She always had some money saved for me to do stuff."

"That's a good idea," Rhyann says cheerfully. "I usually save half of my paycheck and use the other half on clothes or whatever I need and to eat out or see a movie. I guess it's the same thing."

It's a shame. I really want to see Keyshia Cole perform live. I love her music and have her entire album on my MP3 player. She's one of my favorite singers, but concerts and all the eating out that Divine and the girls do—I can't afford it. They have wealthy parents. As for Rhyann, I don't know how she keeps up with them. I just know that I don't have it like that. All I have is Miss Lucy and myself.

"What's got you moping all around the place?" Miss Lucy asks me.

"Nothing."

"I know better than that."

"The girls are going out for dinner tonight. They invited me along, but I turned them down."

"Why didn't you plan to go with them?" Miss Lucy asks.

"I didn't want to spend the money, Miss Lucy. You know that we need to build up our savings for a rainy day."

"Honey, you need to have some fun," she says. "Don't you worry about me. Things are gonna work out—God has my back. I'm seeing a doctor at the VA hospital, and I spoke to someone this morning who told me that my benefits should start up soon. Things gon' be just fine."

"My mama was always counting her chickens before they hatched, as Grandma Ellen used to say. I'm not counting on anything until you get one of those checks. Until then I'm saving every penny."

Miss Lucy laughs. "You think like an old woman. Your grandmother had a strong influence on you."

I don't think it's so funny. "My mama didn't do anything but run the streets. She made it to the eleventh grade, then dropped out of school. She used to do hair at my grandma's house to make money, but that was when she was between men. Whenever she was in love, she forgot about everything and everybody."

Miss Lucy doesn't approve of my tone. "You shouldn't be talking about your mama like that."

"Truth is truth."

The telephone rings.

"Kylie, what are you doing?" Divine asks when I answer.

"Just sitting here talking to Miss Lucy. What's up?"

"We were calling to see if we could come over. We decided since you wouldn't come out with us, we'd come to you and bring the food, too."

I'm delighted, but I don't show it. "You don't have to do that, Divine."

"We want to do it, so can we please come over?"

"Let me ask Miss Lucy."

"Sure," Miss Lucy says before I even mouth the question. "Tell them to come right over."

"She's okay with it."

"Great, we'll be right there. We're not too far from your apartment."

"They're bringing food," I tell Miss Lucy. "I guess we get to eat real good tonight."

"Thank you, Jesus," she moans with her hands up toward the heavens. "I sho' was getting tired of chicken."

I laugh. "Me, too."

When the girls arrive, they greet Miss Lucy and give her hugs.

We sit down at the dining room table. Rhyann pulls out a pack of paper plates, napkins, and plastic ware, while Alyssa opens the containers of food.

"I haven't had seafood in a long time," I say, my mouth watering at the sight of crab legs, shrimp, baked potatoes, cole slaw, garlic biscuits, and even dessert. "This looks so good."

Divine's gaze travels around the apartment. "It's really looking nice in here," she tells me.

I study her expression to see if she's being serious or making fun of our place.

"I'm serious," she says as if she knows what I'm thinking. "I wouldn't mind having something like this when I graduate from college."

"We're going to need a whole house if we all go to college and then live together as we build our careers," Mimi puts in.

Alyssa laughs. "I don't think we're going to be living together that long. I'm marrying Stephen after we graduate college."

"Girl, pleeze," Divine mutters. "Let's eat while the food is hot. I'm starving. You and Stephen may not even be together by then."

"Whatever . . . ," Alyssa replies. "Just because you and Madison didn't make it, don't hate on me and Stephen."

Miss Lucy blesses the food before we all dive in.

The food is delicious. Even Miss Lucy is enjoying the meal.

"What's all that stuff in those bags you brought up here?" I ask Divine, gesturing toward the plastic bags near the door.

Her face brightens like Santa Claus. "My mom made me clean out my closet. I didn't know if you could use any of the stuff, so I brought it with me. Take whatever you want."

"Thank you," I respond, my mouth tightening.

"I brought some stuff for you, too," Mimi says. "Since you and my brother are 'talking,' I thought you might need some dresses to wear when you go out."

I swallow hard, fighting back words of anger. I don't need their hand-me-downs.

"It's not pity or anything, Kylie," Divine quickly adds. "I

have to clean out my closet every summer. Mom will take me shopping for back to school, so it's more of a selfish thing going on. I'm giving to get—I admit it."

"So you'd actually be helping her out," Alyssa says, knowing this is a sore point with me. "That's what my cousin is trying to say. I already shopped in her closet, so ya'll might as well check out what's left." She stabs a fried shrimp with her fork and sticks it in her mouth.

I wipe my mouth with a napkin. "I appreciate y'all thinking of me, but why don't you just take it down to the Salvation Army or Goodwill? There are a lot of people who can use the clothes."

"So you're saying you don't want them?" Mimi asks.

I try to soften the blow. "That's what I'm saying."

"Why not?" she wants to know.

"I don't need your clothes, Mimi. I like what I have in my closet."

"You haven't even looked at any of it."

I get up, wander over to the bags, and pull out clothing. I have to admit that both Divine and Mimi have some beautiful outfits. I check the tags, though, and then turn to Mimi. "Most of this stuff has to be dry-cleaned. I have to save up my money, so I need clothes that I can wash by hand or in a washing machine."

"Oh." Divine looks like she's about to cry. "I didn't think about that."

"It's okay." I'm relieved that this problem lets me off the

hook. "Thanks for thinking of me, but I can't really keep this stuff."

"Maybe you can wear the jeans, though," she tells me.

"Oh yeah," I respond. "I want to keep all those. I can pay you for them." I don't want them giving me anything.

"Kylie, stop that," Divine says as though I said something crazy. "Let me bless you with something." She holds out her arms. "Let's just face facts here—I'm rich. I don't need money. God has blessed my family so that we can be a blessing to others. Now, I'm not going to have you blocking my blessings."

"Amen," Miss Lucy utters. "You heard her, Kylie. You take them clothes. They'll fit you, and as for cleaning them—we'll take care of it. Don't you be blocking no blessings."

I can't believe Miss Lucy is calling me out like that.

"I hope you'll keep the clothes I brought over, too," Mimi says. "Sometimes things don't come out of my mouth right, but I really want to bless you, too."

They both seem sincere, so I say, "I'll keep the clothes. Thank you both."

"Fashion show," Alyssa shouts.

I groan softly. The last thing I want to do is parade the room in clothes that belong to Divine and Mimi.

"It's diva time," Divine contributes. "C'mon, let's see how they fit you."

"Yeah," Rhyann and Mimi say in unison.

"The food is getting cold," I protest.

"C'mon, Kylie . . . pleeze," Divine pleads.

I so don't want to do this.

They keep pleading until I finally give in just to shut them up. I go into the bathroom and slip on a beautiful shirt by some designer named Tahari.

It fits me like a glove. I notice a pair of denim jeans with stitching the color of the shirt. "Okay, y'all want to see what I'm working with?" I yell from the bathroom.

"Yeah," they shout.

I pretend I'm on a runway and parade around the room.

"Girl, you looking good," Rhyann says. "That outfit is cute on you."

"I might need to take that back," Divine says, laughing. "You're looking better than me in those jeans. Kylie, I knew you had some fashionista genes in your DNA somewhere. All right, diva."

I join in. "Whatever . . ."

I try on the rest of the clothes, falling in love with each outfit, but deep down, I know I'm not going to keep them. I'm never going to own such beautiful stuff, so I might as well not get used to wearing it.

"Do you have any movies?" Mimi asks after we go through all of the clothes.

"We do, but you've probably seen all of them," I respond. "We don't buy them until the pre-viewed movies go on sale at Blockbuster. I can get two for twenty dollars."

"I do that, too," Rhyann interjects. "Sometimes they have three for twenty-five."

"Let's see what you have and then we'll pick one," Mimi suggests. "Since we're not going to the movies, I still want to see something. I turned down some quality time with Kyle in favor of my girls, so we need to have a great time."

Rhyann glances over at me and smiles. It means the world to me to be able to spend this evening with Divine, Rhyann, Alyssa, and Mimi.

The only problem is, I don't know what will happen to our friendship if they ever find out about my mom.

Chapter 13

Chandler surprises me the next day by coming to the shop around the time I get off.

"What are you doing here?"

"I wanted to see you," he responds with that cute smile of his. "Do you have a few minutes to take a ride with me? I'll take you home."

"Let me call Miss Lucy to let her know that I won't be coming straight home."

China strolls up to the reception area and says, "Hello, Chandler."

"What's up, China?"

They talk for a few minutes while I gather my things together. Miss Marilee isn't at the salon today, so I'll have to try and speak with her tomorrow.

Chandler drives over to a nearby park. We sit on the swing and talk.

"I really like you, Kylie," he says, looking deep into my eyes. "I want you to know that I'm not trying to run game on you. I've told Mimi how much I care about you."

I press a hand to my chest. "What did she say?"

"What could she really say?" Chandler responds. "She's my little sister—not my girlfriend."

"I know she doesn't want us together."

"She says that she doesn't want us to get together because if something happens, she loses you as a friend."

I can't hide the surprise in my voice. "Mimi actually said that was the reason?"

Chandler nods.

"I was thinking it was because she didn't think I was good enough for you."

"Mimi doesn't want me to hurt you. She actually thought I was nothing but a playa."

"Why did she think that?"

"I used to brag about my girlfriends," he says with a sheepish smile. "I was mostly lying."

"She's still not cool with us talking, though."

"Kylie, I'm crazy about you. I want you to be my girl-friend."

Looking down at my hands, I confess, "I like you a lot, Chandler, but I've never had a boyfriend before. I have to be honest with you. I'm not going to let you get in the way of my studies. And I'm not having sex."

"Okay," he responds with a chuckle. "I'm very clear on where we stand."

"And you still want a relationship with me?"

My breath catches in my throat as Chandler places his hands on my shoulders, and a thrill of anticipation courses through my veins.

I think he's gonna kiss me.

I've never been kissed by a boy.

I tremble as Chandler wraps his arms around me. I'm all nerves. Excitement along with a touch of curiosity thrown in for good measure, as my grandma would say.

He holds me tightly in his arms, pulling me closer and closer into him as we kiss deeply.

Chandler slides his hands under my shirt.

"Whoa . . . ," I say, moving away from him. "The kiss was nice, Chandler, but I'm very serious about this. I don't roll with the other stuff. Slow it down or we're not gonna be able to hang out."

"Kylie, I'm sorry. I just can't help myself. You are too fine."

I dismiss his words with a shake of my head. "Chandler, I like you, but if you're after sex, you might as well move on, because you won't be getting that from me."

He is quiet for a moment. That tells me what I need to know.

"I think you should take me home," I say.

"You don't have to run away from me, Kylie."

"I'm not running away. I just think I need to get home," I insist. "If you don't want to take me, I can catch the bus."

"I told you that I would take you home, and I meant it."

"I hope you're not upset with me."

"I'm not," Chandler tells me. "But, Kylie, I need you to know that I don't sleep with girls I don't have feelings for."

"Chandler, I'm not even thinking in that mind-set," I reply. "We don't know each other that well. We like each other, but I don't think either one of us can say that this relationship will lead to something more serious. It's way too soon."

He's still looking for a way in. "I can agree with that, but you said earlier that we won't ever have sex. Are you one of those girls who don't believe in sex before marriage?"

I hold up my left hand for him to see. "This ring is a purity ring, Chandler. I made a vow to God that I would wait until my wedding night. I intend to keep this promise."

He tries unsuccessfully to hide his disappointment.

"I'm cool with us just being friends," I tell him. "Chandler, I really do like you, but the truth is that I'm not trying to get all serious right now."

"I hear what you're saying and I respect it. But just so you know, Kylie, I'm not giving up on you. I really do care about you."

His words thrill me, but I meant what I said—I'm okay with us just being friends. I'm not gonna let my emotions run wild and end up like my mama.

No way!

"I hope I haven't ruined my chances with you," Chandler says as we walk back to the car.

I break into a smile. "You haven't. As long as you respect me, we're cool."

Chandler pulls up in front of my building, shuts off the car, and gets out, opening the door for me.

"Call me later if you feel like talking."

"Chandler, we're fine," I assure him. "You can call me."

"I hope you don't decide to tell the girl squad what happened. Mimi will be in my face."

"What happens between us is our business," I assure him.

He releases a soft sigh of relief.

Chandler escorts me inside the apartment building. He leaves when I get on the elevator.

"Hey, Miss Lucy," I greet her when I open the door to our apartment.

She's sitting on the couch watching television. "How was your little date with Chandler?"

I break into a short laugh. "It wasn't a date. We just went to a park to talk."

Miss Lucy studies my face. "I think you did a little more than talk. You let that boy kiss you, didn't you?"

I put a hand to my face. "How could you tell?"

She chuckles. "I couldn't. I was just making an educated guess."

I chuckle in my embarrassment. "He's the first boy that ever kissed me."

"Just make sure you two don't get carried away."

"We won't," I say. "Miss Lucy, I can't monkey around like that. I'm not trying to lose my virginity. My grandma used to tell me that it was more precious than gold. It's my only treasure, and I'm keeping it."

Miss Lucy releases a huge sigh of relief. "Thank you, Jesus! That's what I like to hear. Good girl."

As I settle down for the evening, I can't help but wonder if Mimi is being honest with her brother. She and I have never discussed Chandler, but if she is so concerned about me, why doesn't she come to me with her concerns? I'm not so sure I buy her story. I think it's much more than that.

I stroll out of Bank of America, a big grin on my face. I just opened my first savings account with the three hundred dollars I have saved from working at Crowning Glory.

Words cannot fully express how good I am feeling right now. If I hadn't needed so much stuff when we moved in, I probably could've saved a whole lot more.

My happiness deflates when I draw near the beauty shop and see my mama standing outside, smoking a cigarette, looking as hoochie as she always does in a dress that shows off her curvy figure and her huge, heaving bosom. She's so proud of her double Ds and will tell anybody that will listen. I pray that mine won't sprout out like that.

"What are you doing here?" I ask, walking up to her. "Why do you keep coming around? Are you trying to get me fired?"

"How can you go around here telling people that I'm dead?" she demands. "Do you hate me that much that you want me to die?"

My stomach fills with dread. She must have spoken to Miss Marilee, which means she now knows the truth and it didn't come from me. "I don't hate you, Mama. I just thought it was better than telling people the truth."

She places her manicured hands on her hips. "Excuse me?"

"You'd never win mother of the year, but I'm sure you already know that."

"If you know what's good for you, you had better change your tone and quick like. I ain't letting you talk to me any kind of way."

"Mama, I just want peace in my life," I say with a sigh. "I don't want to have to worry about doing my homework in the dark or having to move all the time. You should want more than that for yourself."

"My life is good," she says defensively. "I have a man who pays the bills. You just out here lying to folks and using them."

A wave of anger courses through my veins. I know she didn't just say that! I don't use anybody. That's her MO.

"I'm not using anybody," I retort. "Miss Lucy knows the truth. Miss Marilee . . . I was planning on telling her today, but you've already ruined that for me, so Mama, please go. As you can see, I'm doing okay."

"Since you doing so okay, why don't you help your mama out? I need some money."

"I don't have any to give you."

"I know you, Kylie. You got some money somewhere." She points to the black pants I'm wearing—the ones that Divine gave me—and says, "I know how much Seven jeans cost, so how can you afford them? Are you messing around with a drug dealer?"

"Somebody gave me these."

"Kylie, stop lying," Mama shouts. "That stuff look brand-new. All I'm asking for is a couple of hundred dollars. I gave life to you, so you should want to help me out." She winks at me. "If you got a sugar daddy or something, just tell me. You know I like a man with money."

"I didn't ask to be born," I retort. "And for the record, God gave me life. Not you. I've already told you that I don't have any money. Mama, please . . . don't ruin this for me. Just leave and don't come back here. I have to work in this place, and I don't need to lose my job, if I haven't already. Now that Miss Marilee knows the truth, I may not even have a job."

"Why would you lose your job by me showing up here?"

I don't respond.

"You're ashamed of me, aren't you?"

Tears form in my eyes. "Mama, you never cared about me and I'm tired of you trying to use me. I don't want to disrespect you, but I just want to be left alone. I don't want to live your life anymore."

My words wound her, and she looks like she's about to cry herself. "Kylie, how can you say that I don't care about you?"

"Mama, I have to get to work." I brush past her as fast as I can.

"Come back here, Kylie."

"I have to go," I say, not bothering to look back.

I walk into the hair salon, hoping and praying that Miss Marilee will forgive me. Rhyann, Divine, Alyssa, and Mimi are all standing in the reception area. Before I can explain myself to them, Miss Marilee meets me at the desk. "Is that woman outside your mother?" she asks in a low voice.

A tear slides down my face. "Yes, ma'am. Miss Marilee, I'm so sorry for lying to you. To all of you, but I felt like I didn't really have a choice."

Seeing the look of disappointment on my friends' faces is more than I can bear now, and I can't control my tears any longer.

Miss Marilee takes me by the hand. "C'mon, sweetie. Let's talk in my office."

She closes the door, then takes a seat at her desk. "I think I understand why you didn't tell me the truth about your mother, but I'd like to hear it from you, Kylie. Now, what's really going on, dear?"

"You saw her—my mama. That's how she dresses all the time, and she doesn't like to do anything but party. She doesn't act like a mom is supposed to act. She's not responsible or anything. She is just looking for a man with money, and if she can't find one, she expects me to earn my keep. I don't mind working, but I don't want to give my paycheck over to her if she still won't pay the rent or utilities. Since we've been here, we've been evicted twice and moved four times."

"So you ran away from home?"

She was very patient, but I was upset. "We were gonna lose the apartment and be on the streets or end up living with some man she was seeing." I could feel my throat growing tight. "Miss Marilee, I don't like the way her boyfriends look at me sometimes. The last one before the one she has now—he came into my room one night. I woke up and he was standing there by my bed with no shirt on and just staring at me. When I started screaming for my mother, he ran out of the room."

"You poor dear. Did she put him out?"

I shake my head. "He told her some lie and she just believed him. The only reason she's not with him now is because I think he went to jail. I heard something on the news about his arrest."

"Why do you think she's coming around now? Does she want you to come home, or is it for money?" Miss Marilee asks.

"Yes, ma'am, but I'm not gonna give her my hard-earned money."

"Is she doing drugs?"

"I don't know. She has smoked weed in the past." That awful feeling of fear is coming back. "Miss Marilee, she knows where I live. She and Clyde—that's the new boyfriend—followed the bus and followed me to the apartment."

Her face fills with concern. "Are they harassing you and Lucy?"

"Not really," I say. "They just came by that one time, but I'm sure she'll be back. That's why I didn't want her to know where I live or work."

"I'm so sorry, dear."

"I'm sorry that she's coming around here like this." Sighing, I offer her a way out. "I don't want her starting stuff, so maybe I better just leave. Miss Marilee, can we please stay in the apartment? I'll pay you back for the rent. I have three hundred dollars saved, and I'll work two jobs if I have to. I—"

Miss Marilee interrupts me. "Kylie, you're not going

anywhere. You are my receptionist. If your mother decides to make trouble, then I have no choice but to call my son-in-law. You know Mike is a police officer. Maybe he will be able to talk some sense into them. When you get off, I'll take you home. In the meantime, I need to speak with my attorney regarding your situation, if that's okay with you."

I am so grateful she is sticking up for me. "Thank you so much, Miss Marilee."

China sticks her head inside the office. "Mom, she's back in the salon." She walks all the way inside and gives me a hug. "We love you, Kylie, and I want you to know that we have your back."

"C'mon. Let's get this over with, Kylie." Miss Marilee gives me a hug. "I'll try and talk to your mother."

I release a long sigh. "I don't know if it's gonna help, but you can give it a try."

We walk out into the salon.

"How long you gonna keep me out here waiting like this?" my mama demands in a loud voice.

She's mad for sure now from the look on her face, and I can tell she's about to get rowdy and really humiliate me.

I'm ready to die right here on the spot. I am too embarrassed to hold my head up. There is dead silence in the entire shop because everybody is staring at Serena Sanderson, my mama.

"Serena, I'd like a word with you," Miss Marilee tells her crisply.

"Go on . . . ," she responds, her eyes never leaving me. "What other lies did my ungrateful daughter tell y'all?"

I can feel the heat of her gaze as she tries to stare holes through my body.

"We can talk in my office," Miss Marilee informs her.

Folding her arms across her ample chest, my mama brushes past me and says, "Fine. Ain't gonna change anything, but I'll hear what you have to say." She pauses by me long enough to hiss, "I'ma whup the tar right outta you."

I shrink back, watching her enter the office. Lisa comes over to me and gives me a hug. "It's going to be all right, cutie. Don't you get yourself all worked up." She wipes away the tears drowning my cheeks.

I nod, feeling numb.

I make my way up to the reception area and sit down. Miss Marilee and my mother stay in her office for nearly twenty minutes. When they walk out, I can tell my mama is madder than a rattler with no fangs.

She confronts me. "What have you been telling these people? Why you telling all these lies, huh? Do you hate me this much?"

I meet her gaze straight on. "I don't hate you, Mama, and I didn't tell them anything about you. Remember, they thought you were dead until you decided to come harass me at work."

"Serena, why don't you leave?" Miss Marilee suggests, walking over to the reception desk where we are standing.

"We can meet you later if you'd like to finish this conversation."

Mama glares at Miss Marilee. "I'm not talking to you, lady. What you need to do is stay out of my business! If you don't, you'll be sorry."

"Mama, don't talk to Miss Marilee like that," I say, my voice rising an octave. "She's been nothing but good to me. It's because of her that I even have a place to live. I don't want all this drama, so—"

Mama slaps me hard.

"I know you not trying to take up for this woman," she sputters. "I'm the one who gave you life! You are my child and you will do as I say!"

She tries to grab my arm, but I step out of her reach, my cheek stinging from her slap.

China walks over and stands by her mother. "Miss Thang, you don't go around here disrespecting my mother like that. If you can't act like you have some sense, then you need to leave right now," she warns. "If you don't, I will call the police. Oh, and you don't have another chance to threaten my mother or put your hands on Kylie, because I don't have a problem gettin' with you."

Stunned, my mama doesn't even open her mouth to respond. This is the first time I have ever seen her back down. Given the fierce expression on China's face right now, I wouldn't say a word, either.

Miss Marilee places her arms around me. "Serena, I don't

want this to get ugly, but if you keep acting like this, you will leave me no choice."

My mom puts her hands on her hips and says, "What you gon' do? She my child."

"I keep hearing you say that, but I have yet to see you act like her mother," Miss Marilee responds tersely.

"I just want my daughter to give me some respect." She looks over at me and says, "Kylie, I'm sorry for hitting you like that, but you can't be talking to me any kind of way. I'm sorry."

I don't respond.

"I said I was sorry."

"I heard you," I say after a moment. "The only thing is, you always apologize, then you go and do the same thing all over again." My chest hurts again, and it is getting painful to talk. "Mama, I can't go back to moving every two or three months because you don't do what you're supposed to do."

It's getting so hard to breathe right now, and I'm experiencing this intense feeling of fear. It feels like I'm about to die. I can't explain it any other way except that it's an awful way to feel. My eyes travel past my mama to the door. I pull at the collar of my shirt, saying in a hoarse voice, "I need to get out of here. I can't breathe."

"I got you, dear," Miss Marilee says. "China, take Kylie to my office, please."

"What's wrong with you?" my mama asks. "You high, girl?"

"Your daughter suffers from panic disorder," Miss Marilee announces to her. "I take it that you didn't know. She has them when she's placed under a stressful situation."

I can't hear my mom's response because I'm fighting for air.

China has me count to ten backward, then inhale and exhale slowly. Lisa brings me my anxiety medication and a glass of water.

The attack runs its course. I sit in Miss Marilee's office, welcoming a few minutes alone, away from the drama.

Suddenly, Divine, Alyssa, Rhyann, and Mimi burst into the office, surprising me.

"You okay?" they ask in unison.

"I'm really sorry for lying to y'all," I say, feeling miserable.

"Why didn't you tell the truth?" Rhyann asks. "I can't speak for anyone else, but I would've understood."

"I don't know," I say. "I was planning to tell Miss Marilee the truth today. I was gonna tell y'all, too."

"When?" Rhyann wants to know. "Best friends don't lie to each other, Kylie."

I hang my head. "I'll understand if you don't want to be my friend anymore."

"Our friendship won't end over this, Kylie, but is there anything else you haven't told us?"

"That's it," I say.

"Humph, I would've lied, too, if I had her for a mother," Mimi says.

Divine elbows her. "Not cool, Meems . . . that's Kylie's mom regardless."

"Sorry about that," Mimi tells me.

Alyssa hugs me. "Kylie, I'm so sorry."

"I can't believe she hit you like that," Mimi goes on. "You should file child abuse charges against her."

"Girl, you are too sheltered," Rhyann retorts. "My aunt almost knocked me into next year one time. I was running off at the mouth. I was going so good at it that I started cussing."

Alyssa's eyes widen in her surprise. "I know she got you good. I'd be dead if I'd done something like that to my mama."

"I guess we all tried that at least one time," I say. "But I wasn't disrespecting her this time. I just didn't want her threatening Miss Marilee."

Tears stream down my face. "I know that I'm gonna be fired for sure now. I can't believe she'd make me lose my job like this. I should've just given her the money. Maybe she would've left me alone."

"Your mama would only keep coming back if you gave her money," Rhyann tells me. "That's what usually happens."

"I know," I say. "Do you think Miss Marilee hates me now?"

"No," Rhyann responds. "Trust me, she understands everything."

Divine nods in agreement. "I was in here getting my hair done one time and this chick was running her mouth about Jerome being in prison. Miss Marilee checked her good. She even threatened a photographer one time when he was trying to snap pictures of my mom getting her hair done. It was after her and Ava had that fight."

"I heard about that," I say. "Your mom ended up having to pay for her medical expenses, right?"

"And give her a million dollars."

Mimi stole a peek outside the office. "Your mom and Miss Marilee are standing outside the salon talking."

I stand to my feet. "I'd better get out there. I don't want Mama swinging on Miss Marilee."

"Divine is almost a black belt in tae kwon do, just in case you need her," Mimi informs me.

I leave the office with the girls in tow. They stay inside the shop while I join my mother and Miss Marilee outside.

"You're absolutely right, Serena. Legally, I can't keep your daughter away from you," Miss Marilee is saying. "But the courts are a different story."

"Mama, why are you doing this to me?" I ask. "It's not like you really want me around. You have Clyde."

Mama gives me this wounded deer kind of look. "Why are you trying to make people think that I don't treat you right?"

"That's not what I'm doing," I respond. "I'm just being honest. Miss Marilee, I'm so sorry for telling you that my mama was dead, but it's the way I felt. It was better than telling you the ugly truth."

My mother begins to cry.

I feel bad for hurting her feelings, but I know that it's the right thing to do. "Look, I'm not trying to be mean or to hurt you, Mama. But let's be honest, though—who raised me?"

"I did."

Now who's lying?

My eyes narrow. "Mama . . ."

She turns to Miss Marilee. "We lived with my mother, but it wasn't like I wasn't in the house. I didn't just walk off and leave you, like some folks do."

"Grandma Ellen raised me, and you know it," I say. "I was with her all of the time."

She sighs. "I love my daughter," she tells Miss Marilee. "I was young when I had her, so I did the best I could." Mama looks over at me. "You really happy where you living now?"

I nod. "I'm happier than I've been since leaving Statesville."

"That lady gon' be wanting money or something from me?"

I shake my head.

She starts to give in to what she can't change. "I'ma be checking on you, Kylie. I'ma let things be for right now, but don't think I won't be coming around to check on you. I might not be perfect, but I do love you."

Miss Marilee pulls out a business card. "My numbers are on the back. Call me anytime, Serena."

"You know, I do need a job," she says with a grin. "I can braid hair real good. Can't I, Kylie?"

She's up here talking all loud and even threatening Miss Marilee, and now she wants a job? How ghetto is that?

"Mama . . ."

"I don't have any openings right now," Miss Marilee says. "Kylie's told me how talented you are with hair, though. Have you considered going to cosmetology school?"

Mama shrugs, frowning. "I thought about it, but I don't have the money to do all that."

"You can get financial assistance," Miss Marilee tells her. "Think about it and get back to me. If you want to build a stable home for your daughter, this will give you a chance."

Suspicion fills Mama's face. "Why y'all care so much about my child? Y'all don't know her like that."

"She's a sweetheart," Miss Marilee answers, placing an arm around me. "Why wouldn't we care? Believe it or not, we care about you, too."

She studies me for a moment, then says, "Thanks for taking such good care of my girl."

"Serena, you should be very proud of Kylie. She is responsible, a hard worker, and a very smart girl. She is already planning to go back to school in the fall. She wants to go to college."

"That's good," Mama responds quickly. "I want those things for her, too."

"If you mean that, then show her," Miss Marilee states. "Find employment. Make her feel that she comes first in your life."

My mama eyes me hard. "I guess you'd like it if I were all alone, huh?"

"Mama, I don't want you to be alone, but I also don't want to wake up to a different man every day. You move them in and out like furniture."

A flash of embarrassment shows in her expression. "You don't need to be telling all my business, Kylie."

"Mama, you think people don't already know?" I ask. "People look at the way you dress, the way you act, and all the men coming in and out of our apartment—they know."

"I'm gonna be checking in on you, Kylie," she shoots back.

"Thank you, Mama."

Miss Marilee places a hand on my mother's shoulder. "I'll leave you two alone so that you can talk."

When she goes into the shop, Mama lays into me. "I can't believe you said all that stuff about me. Why you trying to make me look bad?"

"I didn't tell them anything about you, Mama," I remind her. "You're the one who came into the shop telling them that you were my mother."

"I wanted to make sure they were treating you right and that you were getting paid fairly. I was trying to look out for you."

"You wanted to know how much I was getting paid, Mama," I say, just as hard as her. "That's why you been hanging around here—you want money."

I can tell she is upset by my words. "I don't know what my mama was telling you, but I used to give her money all the time. She helped raise you, and I helped her, but I bet she didn't tell you that."

I back off a little. "Grandma Ellen didn't talk bad about you."

Playing with her hair, Mama admits, "I know I could've done better by you, but that's why I was trying to find a good man. I figured if I got married, then I could give you a nice home."

"I would've been happy in any place with you," I say quietly.

"Kylie, it's hard out here. Raising a kid ain't easy for a single mother."

"I know," I respond. "It hasn't been real easy for me, but I'm trying. I have a job and I'll get a second one if I need it. I pay my bills."

My mama's mouth tightens, and I decide this talk is over.

"I need to go back inside to see if I still have a job. Mama, I'm begging you not to come back here to my place of employment. *Please.*"

"Kylie, I shouldn't have slapped you. I'm sorry about that. You a real good kid."

"I'm doing great, Mama. I really am."

She jumps on the softness in my voice. "Are you sure that you can't help me out, Kylie? I just need a few dollars."

I shake my head. "Mama, I can't help you. I don't have any money."

"You're lying," she says. "You store up your money."

"That was before I had a place to live and bills to pay." I glance over my shoulder. I have a feeling that the girls have their faces glued to the window, trying to see what is going on between my mama and me. I really hate that they had to witness this drama.

"Kylie, I thought that old lady was paying for everything. I knew she was using you."

"Miss Lucy is not using me, Mama. We share the apartment and the bills. I don't believe in living with no one for free."

"I guess that's a dig at me," Mama mutters. "Kylie, you think you're so much better than me, but when you grow up, you'll see how hard it is out here."

"Don't you think that a job would help?"

She scoffs at that idea. "A man is supposed to take care of a woman, Kylie. This is the natural order of things. If I'm giving him my goodies, then he shouldn't have a problem paying a bill or two. If he sleeps there, then he should pay the rent."

She's starting to give me a headache. "Mama, I can't talk about this anymore. I have to go back inside and see if I still have a job."

"I'ma go over there to that boutique and wait for Clyde to pick me up," she announces. Then she throws one more thing in my face. "I sho' hope that he got paid today because I need me an outfit for the club tonight."

I'm too disgusted to even bother with a response.

Divine approaches me when I come inside the salon. "Are you okay?"

"As well as can be," I say.

China has been covering for me at the reception desk.

"I'm sorry about all of this," I tell her. "I'm willing to work until closing to make up my time."

"Kylie, this isn't your fault."

"China's right," Miss Marilee says as she joins us. "This has been a trying day for you, dear, so why don't you go on out with your friends—grab a bite to eat and go on home."

"I really don't want to lose any more time," I say.

"Why don't you just plan to work until closing tomorrow, then?"

"Thank you, Miss Marilee," I tell her. "I am so very sorry for everything."

"You don't have to be sorry. Now go on and have some fun."

Mimi takes me by surprise when she grabs my hand. "We know just what you need."

"What?" I ask.

"Ice cream sundaes!" she and Alyssa say in unison.

"I want to be the one to tell Chandler the truth, Mimi," I say.

She nods.

Miss Marilee gives Rhyann the rest of the evening off so that she can join us. She and I both will be working tomorrow until closing.

Girls just wanna have fun.

Chapter 14

Chandler arrives promptly at seven.

"The reason I asked you over here is because I need to tell you something," I say. I'm not sure how Chandler is going to feel about me when he finds out that I'm a big fat liar.

He scans my face. "Kylie, what's wrong?"

We sit down on the sofa. "I haven't been totally honest with you, Chandler."

His smile disappears. "About what?"

I take a deep breath and exhale slowly. "I lied about my mother. She isn't dead."

Chandler's eyes widen. "She isn't?"

"No, she's alive and well. She came to my job today and completely embarrassed me. The girls have been very supportive, but I know that they're upset with me for lying to them."

"Wow, Kylie," he says. "That's a pretty big lie."

"I know. I'm an awful person."

Chandler reaches over and takes my hand in his. "No, you're not. You're just in a bad place. But you shouldn't go around telling people that your mom is dead."

"I know all that," I fire back at him. "Chandler, I'm sorry for snapping at you. I'm just stressed out."

"What's going on between you and your mom?"

I tell him more about what my life has been like.

"Wow," he mutters. "I guess my dad working too much is not something I should be complaining about."

"It can go from one extreme to the other, I guess."

Chandler agrees.

"My life would be so much better if only my mother would leave me alone," I tell him. "She has already embarrassed me enough. I'm going to the library tomorrow. I intend to research how to emancipate myself so that I won't have to deal with her."

He is shocked by this idea. "Are you sure you want to do that?"

"I'm basically taking care of myself now," I say. "Why shouldn't I do it?"

"Hey, I'm on your side, Kylie. I just want you to give this some more thought. That's a big step."

No kidding. "I don't have any other choice, Chandler."

The girls go with me to the library two days later, but we are unable to find what I am looking for, so Rhyann suggests that we just search the Internet, which is how we end up at Mimi's house.

Chandler is out playing basketball with some friends. I'll probably be gone before he comes home, which is fine, because I get the feeling that he doesn't think I'm doing the right thing.

After a long time of hunting on the 'Net and finding only a bunch of legal stuff we couldn't understand, I push away from the desk and blurt in frustration, "I think what I really need to do is get a lawyer. That's the best way for me to find out what my rights are."

"Why do you need a lawyer?" Mimi asks. "You don't live with your mother, and you said that she's not exactly a nice person. What can she do to you?"

"That's just it, Mimi," I say. "I don't know what she can do. All I know is that I don't want to be forced to live with my mom and Clyde. The only way I can avoid that is to be emancipated."

"Who's Clyde?" Alyssa asks.

"He's my mama's boyfriend."

Mimi holds up her hand. "Let's back up. What do you mean, you have to be emancipated? Weren't we emancipated like a long, long time ago? I thought Lincoln took care of that for us."

Rhyann gives Mimi a gentle nudge. "Shut up."

"It means that I'd be legally independent of my mama," I explain. "This way my mama doesn't have any say in what I do."

"Can you do that?" Alyssa asks. "You don't have to be eighteen?"

"No," I respond. "I did some research, and the law says that I have to be at least sixteen years old and meet certain conditions. For example, I would have to be married or in the military or be living apart from my parents and managing my own money. Well, I fit the last one like a mouse to cheese."

"Okay, so how do you become emancipated?" Mimi wants to know.

"I have to file or have a lawyer file a petition for emancipation with the court. I want it done right, so that is why I need to get an attorney. I think that I might be able to have one appointed for free, but I figure if he doesn't have a dog in this fight, he won't work too hard. If I pay for one, then he'll work that much harder for me."

I pick up my soda and take a sip. "After I file, there will be a hearing in front of a judge to talk about the emancipation petition. After he hears what we have to say, he rules. If I'm emancipated, I can get my own place to live or stay with Miss Lucy if I want."

"I might have to use that idea the next time my mother goes off into serious Mom mode," Divine says with a chuckle.

I give Divine a sidelong glance. "Think about it. You won't be under the control of your parents, but remember that it works both ways. They don't have to support you financially, give you food, clothing, or a place to live. You're responsible for everything—just like a grown-up."

Mimi frowns. "Are you sure you really want to do this, Kylie?"

She sounds just like her brother.

"It's not like I really have a choice, Mimi," I say. "I'm already on my own, so I might as well make it legal. I want to stay with Miss Lucy. We need each other. I don't want my mama ruining that."

"I can call Mother. She will get you a list of the top lawyers here in L.A.," Mimi suggests.

"Mimi, I can't afford a top lawyer," I say with a thread of irritation. "I probably need one who just graduated law school and barely passed the bar on the tenth time. That's if I'm lucky. The one I get will most likely be slower than molasses trying to run uphill in January."

Divine and Rhyann burst into laughter.

"I'm serious," I say. "I have enough money for him to tell

me everything I need to know in one hour, so he's gonna need to talk quick."

Mimi opens her purse and pulls out a credit card. "We can use this. Let's call a lawyer and talk to him or her."

"I can't—"

She stops me. "Kylie, I know that we have some issues where my brother is concerned, but we'll sort through all that later. Right now we need to figure out something. Whether you believe it or not, you're my girl, and we have to look out for each other. That's how it works in the fab five B.F.F. club."

"I have some money in my savings," Divine chimes in. "If you really want to do this, Kylie, then let us help you. You're one of us, like Mimi said, and we are not about to let you go through this alone."

I'm touched, but I don't want to be dependent on my friends. "I appreciate what y'all trying to do, but I don't want to owe anybody."

"You won't owe me a thing," Mimi responds as if she knows what I'm thinking.

"How will you explain all this to your parents?" I ask. "They will see the credit card bill."

"I won't have to," she replies. "My parents don't see the statements—they go straight to our accountant. But I'll tell Mother about it." She brightens up, running with the thought. "I'm telling you, she won't mind. She'd be proud of me for helping out a friend. Now let's get you that attorney."

I shake my head. "I can't let y'all do this for me. I'm sorry. I'll figure something out."

"Kylie, you need to stop letting your pride get in the way," Rhyann tells me.

I let my anger get the best of me. "What? Does it make y'all feel good to help out the poor homeless girl?"

They stare at me, speechless.

"You forced your clothes on me, and now you're forcing money on me. I said I didn't want your help."

"See, that's the problem," Divine says with frustration in her voice. "You see yourself as the poor homeless girl. We don't see you that way, Kylie. We are just trying to be a friend to you. We have tried to understand your situation, even why you lied to us about your mother."

She really went there with me.

"You didn't have to keep the clothes, and you don't have to accept our help, but you don't have to be mean to us for trying to be good friends."

My eyes fill with tears. "It makes me feel bad," I say. "Divine, I'd like to be able to help myself."

"One day you will be able to, but don't you think that God placed you in our lives for a reason?"

"I'm sorry for sounding so ungrateful," I say, wiping my eyes with my hands. "This is really stressing me out." I can feel my chest tightening as I talk. "That's when I have these attacks."

Rhyann begins rubbing my back. "Slow down your breathing, Kylie."

Tears run down my cheeks. "I hate going through this drama. All I want is a normal life."

Alyssa takes my hand, and she begins to pray for me. I pray along with her because I really need God to help me through this.

When she is done, Alyssa says, "The Bible tells us that by Jesus' stripes we are healed. We all have to agree that Kylie is gonna be healed from these anxiety attacks."

"Kylie, we don't want to make you feel bad, but the truth is that you need some help right now," Mimi says. "Please let us help you with the attorney. We hate seeing you so upset. I don't know if you've ever had real friends, but having each other's back is part of the B.F.F. code."

I glance over at Rhyann, who agrees. "We want to help you, Kylie, simple as that."

I really do need a lawyer, I tell myself. Maybe it won't hurt to accept help from the girls this one time. "Are you sure about this?"

"Yeah," they say in unison.

"Good," Divine tells me. "Let's start with my mom's attorney. She's really nice."

Chapter 15

My mother is waiting at the bus stop for me when I step off the bus the following week. I met with the attorney, and Divine was right about Diane Jenkins. She was really nice and counseled me on what it truly means to be an emancipated teen. Then she gave me the cost of her services.

I managed to keep a straight face, thank her, and get out of her office as fast as I could. There was absolutely no way I could afford Diane Jenkins.

The girls were waiting in the lobby for me.

"How did it go?" Divine asked.

"Too expensive," I replied. "Let's get out of here before she charges me for standing in the reception area."

Now I was face-to-face with the person I wanted to be emancipated from. "Mama, I need to get to work."

She is determined to follow me. "I hate to ask, but I really need some money, Kylie. Clyde and I had a fight, and he moved out without paying the bills. My lights about to be cut off and there is no food in the apartment. The lights are in his name 'cause I still owe money. Kylie, you know if they get turned off, I can't get them back on unless I put them in somebody else's name."

"I don't have any money," I respond, "and I can't get any lights in my name. You already messed me up with that."

"I don't want you to get the lights in your name, Kylie. I just want to get the bill paid. Can't you get it from that lady you living with or Miss Marilee? I know that they would give you just about anything."

I shake my head. "Mama, I can't do that."

She grabs me roughly by the arm. "*Why not?* If they want you so bad, they can pay me."

I snatch my arm away from her. "Mama, I can't believe that you just said that," I cry, my heart breaking into pieces. "Now you're willing to sell me—the daughter that you claim to love so much. I'm not trying to disrespect you, but why don't you get a job? Then you can pay your own bills."

She tosses her long curly weaved hair over her shoulders. "You owe me, Kylie Sanderson."

I'm not about to let her guilt me. "I don't owe you anything. I owe Grandma Ellen, if anybody. She is the one who took care of me," I state. "When I was with her, I had a home and I never had to worry about food, lights, or a roof over my head. I didn't have panic attacks until we moved out here."

My mother mutters a string of profanities before saying, "I'm so tired of you saying that stuff. Yeah, my mom helped me out from time to time with you, but I did the best that I could, Kylie."

"Do you actually believe that living off men is what's best for me?" I ask. "Mama, look at you. You walk around wearing little skimpy outfits that barely cover your body. Do you really think I like men ogling you all the time—even the boys my age? Nobody needs to see that much of you, and if that is not embarrassing enough, you came out here wanting to dance in music videos. I don't know any moms who want to do that."

"Kylie, what's wrong with me wanting to be an actress? Why should I have to give up my dream?"

"Have you even gone on one audition?" I ask, folding my arms across my chest. "Have you taken one acting class?"

"No, I need some new clothes for that," my mama responds. Then a sly look comes into her eyes. "See, if you help me out this one time, I can pay you back when I get my first acting job."

I switch my backpack from one side to the other and check my watch. "Mama, I need to get to work. I don't want to be late."

She begins to plead her case some more. "Kylie, I really need some help. You don't want me to be hungry, do you? Can't I just come to your place and stay for a few days?"

The realization hits me square in the face. That is what she really wanted. "No, Mama." I begin walking fast toward the salon.

Mama follows me, hustling to keep up. "How can you be so cold to me?"

"I'm not trying to be cold. I'm just trying to get by, Mama."

She's not about to give up, so she throws in, "Kylie, I didn't want to come to you like this, but I really need your help."

That breaks through the barrier I've put up. Just as I am about to pull out the ten dollars I have in my pocket, her cell phone rings.

"Hey, baby," she murmurs. "I know . . . I'm trying . . . I gotta go."

Disgusted, I break into a run.

I cannot believe I almost fell for her lies. The way she's acting, I'm beginning to wonder if she is using drugs. I can smell marijuana on her this morning. I'm not about to give her money for weed or drugs.

I make it to work just minutes before my shift begins.

Miss Marilee studies my face and says, "You saw your mother?"

"How did you know?"

"I saw her when I was driving in this morning. I had hoped she would take off before you arrived, but I guess she didn't."

"She met my bus."

Miss Marilee shakes her head sadly.

Mimi walks through the door, her cell phone glued to her ear. She waves at me. I check her in while she takes a seat.

A few minutes later, she ends her call and comes up to the reception desk. "I had to talk to my boo. He's missing me."

China comes up front to get Mimi.

Half an hour later, Chandler surprises me by coming up to the shop.

"What are you doing here?" I ask. "Your sister is here getting her hair done."

"I thought I'd come by and take you to lunch," he responds with that beautiful smile of his. "As for Mimi, I hope she already ate, because she's not invited."

I grin. "She may be under the dryer by now, but she hasn't been here that long."

"Can you leave now?"

Lisa walks up to the front and says, "I'll relieve you, Kylie. My next client won't be here until two."

I thank her and grab my wallet.

We decide to eat at the sandwich shop across the street. My gaze travels to the trash area where I used to look for cans. I see a woman over there searching for edible scraps and cans.

"Hold up a minute," I say to Chandler.

I walk over and ask, "Would you like a sandwich and something to drink?"

She eyes me for a moment before nodding.

"I'll buy you a sandwich. What would you like?"

She looks at me like I have lost my last mind, but when I meet her gaze, I say, "My name is Kylie. I used to be homeless."

"Ham and cheese," she tells me. "No onions."

I smile. "I'll be right back, so please don't leave."

"That's nice of you," Chandler says.

We order our food, and I get a sandwich, a bag of chips, and a soda for the homeless lady outside. We pay and leave.

"Here you are," I say. "I didn't know if you wanted white or wheat, so I picked white."

"God bless you for your kindness."

"Go to the Safe Harbor Mission," I tell her, noticing her bruises. "They will keep you safe."

Chandler hands her a five-dollar bill. "Here's some money for the bus. If they won't let you on, find the nearest policeman and ask him to take you to the mission."

"You can even call the mission and they'll send someone to pick you up," I add. "I had to stay there for a while, and they were real nice. They don't just give you three hots and a cot, they also give you hope."

"Your heart is good and generous," the woman says with tears in her eyes. "God wants me to impart something into your life. He wants you to be this way with everyone. Look past the outside to the heart deep within, child of God. In order to be forgiven, you have to forgive. May you continue to be blessed beyond measure."

I have no idea what she's talking about, but I smile and nod anyway.

The woman thanks us again, then makes her way to the bus stop.

"I hope the bus driver doesn't treat her bad," I say. "They don't always want you on their bus."

Chandler eyes me from head to toe, and he likes what he sees. "I still can't believe you were once homeless."

"That's the thing with people, Chandler. They think they are so removed from it, as if it can't happen to them. The truth is that not all homeless people are druggies or have mental problems. They are normal people like you and me. They look like us—just in a bad way."

He nods in understanding.

We go back inside the salon.

Mimi's expression changes when she sees her brother with me. I ignore her and take Chandler to the break room.

"Let's do something this evening," Chandler suggests while we're eating our lunch. "We could check out a movie or have dinner somewhere."

"I have to check in with Miss Lucy, so can I call you later?" I ask him. "She wasn't feeling too well this morning." I bite into my sandwich.

"Yeah, that's fine."

"I'm pretty sure it won't be a problem," I say. "I just want to make sure she doesn't need me there with her. If it's a go, let's do a movie, because I want to see the new one with Beyoncé."

"Okay," Chandler responds.

China is almost done with Mimi's hair when I walk her brother back to the front. "I see your sister is still tripping over us talking."

He shrugs in nonchalance. "I don't care and you shouldn't, either." As if to prove a point, he leans over and kisses me on the lips. "I'll see you later."

I turn around to find Mimi standing there.

"I guess you two are getting pretty tight," she tells me.

"Mimi, I'm not going down this road with you. I have a job to do." I step around her. "Thanks again for helping me with the lawyer."

Chapter 16

"Hey, Dee called me earlier," Rhyann tells me the next day. "We're going to the mall after work, and then grab something to eat. I hope you'll go with us this time. You always say no."

I release an impatient sigh. "Rhyann, I keep telling you, I don't want to go and be the only one who can't shop or pay for those expensive meals y'all always buying. I don't have it like that," I tell her. "I can't throw away money on clothes for the fun of it."

"Okaay," she mutters. "I guess that's a no, then. You know, Kylie, your attitude is really beginning to suck."

"Rhyann . . ."

She walks off before I can apologize for snapping.

I feel awful, because I never meant to go off on Rhyann. When I get a break, I make my way to the shampoo bowl.

"Rhyann, I'm so sorry for snapping at you like that," I tell her. "I didn't mean what I said about the clothes. It's really not my business how y'all spend your money."

"It's cool, Kylie," Rhyann replies coolly. "I know that you've been under a lot of stress, but you need to stop tripping like that. We're your friends—at least we're trying to be. You have to lighten up some."

We walk into the break room and sit down at the table. "I really do like hanging with y'all, but Rhyann, I don't have money like that, and even if I did, I don't think I'd be buying all those expensive clothes. I'm cheap, and I like being this way."

"That's not being cheap, Kylie," Rhyann points out. "You're just being wise with your money. Humph! I go to the mall, but I don't spend money like Mimi and Divine. I don't know if you ever noticed, but Alyssa doesn't either, Kylie. We just go to hang out with our friends. Nobody is going to make you feel bad if you're not a slave to all things designer. I'm like you—I'm trying to save a little money."

"Since we're talking about this, Rhyann, I don't want

people always paying for me. I've seen my mama take advantage of so many people," I tell her. "I don't want to be anything like her. I'm not a user."

"I know that," Rhyann responds. "Girl, we all know that about you. That's why you're now an official B.F.F. and entitled to full privileges."

"Well, butter my tail and call me a biscuit," I say, grinning from ear to ear. "I got me some B.F.F.'s."

Rhyann laughs loudly. "Kylie, first rule of a B.F.F.—never say that butter thingy again. NEVER."

I'm so bored just following the girls around as they try on this blouse and those pants. Mimi's wrist should be hurting from all the times she's whipped out her credit card.

You would think that she didn't own a stitch of clothing in her closet from the way she's shopping. Divine isn't a slouch, either, when it comes to trying on just about everything. I stand beside Alyssa and try to stifle a yawn.

She glances over at me and laughs. "What's wrong with you, Kylie? Are you tired from all the window-shopping?"

"More bored than anything else," I respond honestly.

Mimi gasps in shock. "What kind of person are you, Kylie? Who doesn't like to shop?"

I try to remain patient. "Mimi, we've been in this mall for two hours. You only have two hands—how much can you carry? You already bought out the last store."

"You haven't bought anything, so you can help carry some of my stuff."

"NOT."

Mimi stares at me. "Kylie, what is your problem?"

"You two, don't start," Rhyann quickly interjects. "We're supposed to be having a good time."

"Kylie, if you didn't want to be here, then you shouldn't have come," Mimi tells me. "I'm so tired of feeling bad that I'm not poor."

"Yeah, right," I answer wearily. "The last thing you'd ever want is to walk in my shoes. You'd have a meltdown."

"Kylie, you have no right to judge me. I can't help it if my parents are wealthy and I benefit from it."

"You think you're so much better than me."

"No, *you* think I'm better than you," she retorts. "You don't think you're good enough to be our friend, and while everyone else is too polite to tell you, I'm not. Kylie, this is really getting on our nerves. *Stop being a freaking victim.*"

I'm too stunned by her words to respond.

"What Mimi is trying to say is that we like you for you, Kylie," Divine puts in. "But sometimes you make it difficult by putting up a wall between us—that wall is your circumstances. Now, Mimi can be snobby at times. Me, too, but we accept you as you are. The problem is that you seem to want us to change who we are, and well, that's totally not going to happen."

I can't believe they are trying to turn this all around on

me. "You know what? This was a bad idea." I look toward the mall's entrance. "I'm going to take the bus home."

"There's that wall again," Divine says.

"Well, guess what?" I say snidely. "You don't have to deal with it anymore. This friendship is not going to work." I rush off before they can see the tears run down my face. I keep telling myself, *I don't need them—or anyone else, for that matter.*

Chapter 17

I find my mama waiting for me outside the apartment building when I arrive home. How can my life become any more miserable?

"What are you doing here?"

"I came to see you," she says tightly. "I miss my daughter. Anything wrong with that?"

I survey her face. "I'm not sure I believe you, Mama. I think you want something."

Just then Miss Lucy walks up. She isn't surprised to see my mama. "I see you're back, Serena."

"Kylie, I need to talk to you." Mama eyes Miss Lucy, then adds, "Alone."

Miss Lucy stays right where she is. "I'm not going anywhere."

Mama glares at Miss Lucy for a moment, then turns her attention back to me. "I have some stuff in the car," Mama says. "I need to stay here with y'all. It's just a few days, Miss Lucy, if you don't mind."

I shake my head. "Mama, I'm sorry, but you can't stay here. I don't know what's going on with you, and to be honest, I really don't want to know."

She starts crying. "I got evicted, Kylie. What am I supposed to do?"

"Pay your rent," I retort angrily. "Mama, this is what you always do, and then you look for someone to bail you out." I'm not giving in on this point. "We don't have room, and we don't have permission."

"Don't nobody needs to know that I'm staying here."

"Miss Marilee owns this building," I tell her. "She would know that you're here because I'm not gonna lie to her anymore, and neither is Miss Lucy."

"I have nowhere to live," she shouts.

Passersby strolling along the sidewalk stop and stare until my mama gets ghetto and says, "What y'all looking at? This ain't your business, so just keep on moving."

"You can go to a shelter, Mama."

"I can't believe you're being so coldhearted."

I can't let her words hurt me anymore. I know that I have to be firm. "Mama, I'm really not trying to hurt you—I'm just telling you the truth. It's time for you to grow up and be responsible. This is exactly why I want to be emancipated. I love you, Mama, but I just can't do this with you anymore. You're on your own."

I leave her standing on the sidewalk and go inside the building. She's still standing outside when I get on the elevator.

"You were pretty hard on your mother just now," Miss Lucy tells me as we enter our apartment.

Dropping my purse on the sofa, I say, "I told her the truth. She needs to get a job. I think it might do her some good to stay in a shelter for a while."

"Are you trying to punish your mother?"

"No, ma'am. I just want her to help herself for once in her life. Miss Lucy, do you think I'm wrong?"

Her voice betrays some doubt. "No, I don't. I just want to make sure you're doing this for the right reason. We probably could've let her stay here one night."

I shake my head. "My mama wasn't gonna leave. I know her, Miss Lucy. Once she got in here, she would try to stay here as long as she could. I don't like being this way with her, but my grandma used to always say that Mama needed tough love."

I really hope that this will help her get her life together.

I tell Miss Marilee about my mother's visit when I come to work on Tuesday.

"I'm sure it must have hurt you to do that to your mother, but I think you made the right decision. Your mother does need to get a job so that she can make it on her own."

"Then why do I feel so terrible?"

"Because you're human and you have a merciful heart."

"I really love my mother, Miss Marilee. I do. All I want is for her to get it together. She wants me to respect her. I feel that she needs to earn that respect."

It seems like I've gone too far, because Miss Marilee strikes the same note Miss Lucy did. "Kylie, she's your mother, and I know that you honor her because of that fact," Miss Marilee says. "Being a parent doesn't come with a handbook, so I want you to consider giving Serena a break. She was only fourteen when she had you, dear. Younger than you are now."

"I know that," I say, bowing my head.

"If you were to have a child right now, do you think that you could do any better than your mother?"

I take a seat in the chair behind the counter. "Actually, I do," I tell Miss Marilee. "I'd work two or three jobs to take care of my child. I wouldn't be dependent on a man for nothing."

Miss Marilee leans on the counter. "So when would you have time for your child with all of those jobs?"

I think about her question. "I would have to work in order to take care of my child. I want to give my children everything I didn't have. I—"

Miss Marilee cuts me off. "Do you know what children want most, Kylie?"

"What?"

"Love and quality time."

I nod in understanding. "I get it now, Miss Marilee. Sure, that's what I've wanted from my mama all this time. Now I see that there's more than one way to mess up as a parent. Sometimes you can focus too much on your job and not be there for your child."

"You have to find a balance, and for some parents it's not an easy task. Then to be fourteen on top of that . . . just think about what I've said."

Miss Marilee's words weigh heavily on my mind throughout the rest of my day.

Rhyann comes to work around noon. We say hello, but that's about it. I can tell she's still upset over the words exchanged at the mall the other day. I consider going to the shampoo area and apologizing to her, but I don't, because I don't feel I was wrong.

Yet I already miss the girls, and I have not really talked to Chandler, either. I just have to keep my distance from all of them. I know this is for the best, because I'm not rich.

But why does it have to hurt so much?

Chapter 18

T he girls arrive shortly after I get home from work.

"We seriously thought about kicking you to the curb, Kylie," Rhyann tells me, "but we decided to come over here and talk this thing out once and for all."

"Just so you know, we don't go chasing down people. We have lots of friends," Mimi adds. "People who *want* to be our friends."

"Not really helping, Mimi," Divine says to her.

"Maybe she's right," I say, discouraged. "We come from different backgrounds—too different to be friends."

"That's a load of bull and you know it," Rhyann says. "Kylie, Alyssa and I don't have rich parents. My mother is dead and I live with my aunt. Divine's parents are divorced, so she has a blended family. Mimi's parents are still together, but her father has a son with an ex-girlfriend. Why are you tripping like this?"

"Y'all are trying to act like I have the problem, but it's not me. Mimi doesn't really like me and I know it. I see all the strange looks you give me, especially when I'm with Chandler."

"You think I don't want you with Chandler because you're not good enough," Mimi responds. "That's not even the case, Kylie. I don't want him hurting you, and then it affects our friendship. I had that happen one time already with Chandler."

"Kylie, if my girls weren't cool, I never would've introduced you to them," Rhyann tells me. "The other day, you saw I only bought one shirt, and it was marked down to eight dollars. I don't feel bad because I can't shop like Dee or Mimi."

"It definitely don't bother me," Alyssa says. "We really want to be friends with you, Kylie."

"Why?" I ask. I wave my hand around our itty-bitty apartment. "Why do you want to be friends with me?"

"Because you're brave," Mimi says. "Kylie, I could never handle something like this. I'd die."

Divine nods in agreement. "We admire you, and while

you aren't a fashionista, you're still very cool. We have fun and we enjoy being around you."

"Until you start tripping," Rhyann adds.

Divine says something she obviously had planned to say. "We promise not to force you to go on our shopping sprees if you don't want to go. We're just so used to doing almost everything together."

They are so nice, and I'm feeling a lot better that they think enough of me to have come over. "I guess I was a little jealous because I just can't shop anytime I feel like it," I confess. "I like spending time with y'all, but it did make me feel like an outsider."

"You're not an outsider, Kylie," Mimi tells me. "We're all different, and yes, I'm shallow at times, but this is me. Love me or hate me."

I smile.

"Friends?" Mimi asks, holding out her hand to me. "For real this time."

I shake her hand. "For real."

We do a fabulous five group hug.

"I'm glad y'all got that straight," Miss Lucy says from the kitchen.

Rhyann holds up her sleeping bag. "I called Miss Lucy earlier, and she said that it was fine for us to kick it over here for the night. We wanted to surprise you."

"You're staying here?" I ask, grinning from ear to ear. "Like a slumber party?"

"Yeah," they respond in unison.

I can't believe they actually want to stay here with me in this tiny little apartment, but that's okay with me.

"I have a great idea," I say.

All eyes on me, they ask in unison, "What?"

"We can make something, like nachos. Chips, chicken, cheese, salsa, olives, black beans, jalapenos—the works."

Mimi frowns. "Girl, I do not know how to cook, and I have no interest in learning."

"Then stay away from the chicken," I say with a chuckle. "You just man the salsa. I'll cook the chicken."

"I'll handle the chips," Mimi counters. "Let Rhyann do the salsa. She makes it homemade, and it's delicious."

I glance over at Rhyann. "You can make salsa?"

She nods. "I just need some tomatoes, garlic, green chilies, onions, cilantro, lime juice, olive oil, and jalapenos."

"You make it like we do, then," I respond. "We have all of that stuff."

Alyssa follows me to the kitchenette. "I want to see how you do the chicken."

"I take skinless chicken breasts and poach them, and after they cool, I shred the meat with my fingers."

Divine joins us. "What do you want me to do?"

"Can you cut up the lettuce?"

She nods. "I'll help Rhyann cut up the stuff she needs for the salsa, too."

Mimi rises to her feet. "I'm going to run to the store and get more chips and some soda. I can tell you right now, that one bag isn't going to be enough for all of us. Kylie, they might not look or act like it when we're in a restaurant, but these divas can eat." She grabs her purse. "Do you need anything else?"

"I don't think so." I glance over at Miss Lucy. "Do you need anything?"

"Mimi, if you don't mind, can I ride to the store with you? I need to pick up my meds."

"I don't mind at all, Miss Lucy."

"Oh, my goodness!" Divine exclaims thirty minutes later. "This is the best chicken nachos I've ever eaten. That queso sauce is delicious!"

"Kylie, what else can you make?" Mimi asks, licking her lips. "I think I'm going to be hanging out over here."

"We could do a low country boil," I say. "We only did it once so far, and that was to celebrate Miss Lucy getting her benefits and having this apartment. I make fried chicken, liver and onions, macaroni and cheese—all sorts of stuff. I've been cooking since I was nine."

"All of that sounds good," Rhyann says. "Okay, when we get to college, Kylie is my roommate. I called it first."

"Rhyann, you can cook, so you don't need Kylie. I can't boil water, so she has to be my roommate," Mimi argues. "I'll just live with you both."

"Yeah, let Mimi stay with y'all," Alyssa says with a chuckle. "Divine is enough high maintenance for me. I don't need two of them."

"I might be a year behind y'all," I remind them. "I'm

gonna try, but there's no guarantee that I'ma be able to catch up all of my credits in order to graduate on time."

"That's not a big deal," Mimi states. "We'll get a three-bedroom apartment so you'll have a room when you get there, or we can just have our mothers rent a five-bedroom house for us so we can all live together. What do you think? Won't that be cool?"

"We could split the rent five ways," Rhyann responds.

Divine nods in approval. "I like that idea."

We continue discussing our plans for college as we finish off the nachos. Alyssa and I clean the kitchen while Divine wipes down the table. Rhyann and Mimi sit on the sofa going through a stack of movies.

I jump at the sound of the doorbell ringing.

Miss Lucy walks out of the bathroom and says, "I'll get it."

My chest tightens at the thought of my mother standing on the other side of the door. The girls and I are having a good time, and I don't want her to come and ruin everything for me.

I relax when Miss Marilee walks through the front door.

"Is there a party and nobody told me about it?" she inquires with a grin.

"You're welcome to hang out with us," I say. "We made some chicken nachos earlier, but we ate it all."

"Maybe next time," she says. "I actually came over to rescue Lucy. We are going out for a nice quiet dinner, and then we're going to catch a movie. You girls behave while we're gone."

"We will," we say in unison.

I'm thrilled to see Miss Lucy getting out and enjoying herself. She needs to do that more often instead of always looking out for me. She's totally opposite of my mama, that's for sure.

In another few minutes, Chandler calls me. I go into the bathroom to chat with him in private for a few minutes.

"I'll call you back later. The girls are here now."

"Oh yeah," he says. "I forgot Mimi went to your place. Call me back."

"I will."

I open the door to the bathroom.

Divine, Rhyann, and Mimi are practically facedown on the floor. Alyssa doubles over in laughter.

"What are y'all doing?" I can't control my laughter. "That's what you get for being so nosy."

They laugh.

"I can't believe you busted us like that," Rhyann tells me.

"I can tiptoe softer than a mosquito. Miss Lucy and I live in real close quarters, so we try to be quiet around here. Now that y'all got your faces all cracked, let's go watch the movie."

"All right now . . . ," Mimi murmurs. "My brother's got it going on . . ."

My face heats up.

"Don't be shamed," Alyssa tells me. "Having a boyfriend is great. I don't know what I'd do without Stephen."

"I don't want Chandler to become my entire world," I say.

"I know that's right," Rhyann contributes. "Girls, we have to stay focused so we can get our tails in college."

"So, are you completely over Madison?" Mimi asks Divine.

"I am," she responds. "At first I was really hurt, and I felt the same sadness I used to feel when I lived out here."

"Your life is perfect, Divine," I interject. "I can't really imagine why you'd ever be sad about anything."

Her smile disappears. "Girl, my life sucks sometimes just like everybody else's. It might look all glamorous to other people, but it was not like that. When my parents were married, we were miserable. Jerome was cheating on my mom and treating her bad. On top of that, he was always getting himself arrested for something—I was so embarrassed. It was not until I moved in with my aunt and uncle that I realized this was Jerome's problem and not mine. I had to forgive him, and when I got to the point where I could, that's when I could hold my head up. You have to get to that place with your mom."

"I understand what you're saying," I tell Divine. "My mama has gotten herself in trouble with the law a few times, too. I just want to be a normal teen."

"I know that's right," Rhyann throws in. "We're supposed to be enjoying our youth and not having to deal with a bunch of drama."

I pick a pillow off the sofa and clutch it to my chest. "I have to be real honest with y'all. I still don't know why you'd want to be my friend. My life is on the crazy side thanks to my mama."

"It's not your fault. We don't get to pick our parents, Kylie." Rhyann embraces me. "We love you just because you're you, and together we'll get through whatever you have to deal with."

I smile. "I feel the same way about y'all."

"You and I are a lot alike," Divine tells me. "I never approved of my dad's lifestyle. At one time, I really thought that I hated Jerome."

"How did you mend your relationship?"

"I gave him another chance to get it right."

"Was this before he went to prison?"

Divine shakes her head. "This all happened while he was incarcerated. Kylie, I had to forgive him."

My face darkens at that thought. "I don't know how to forgive my mama. Every time that I think I can, she does something else to me."

"Kylie, I hope you won't get mad at me, but I have to say this because I've been there. You may not approve of your mother's lifestyle, but you have to forgive her."

I hear what Divine is saying. I am just not sure I can ever forgive my mama.

The next morning, we wake up to Divine's excited chirping. She drops her cell phone, saying, "We have backstage passes to see Mary J. Blige. My mom got us passes."

"That's nice," I say, rubbing my eyes. "I hope y'all have fun."

"Kylie, you're going with us," Divine announces. "She got enough for all of us to go."

My eyes fill with tears. "Are you serious? I'm actually gonna be backstage at a Mary J. Blige concert?"

Divine nods, a huge grin on her face. "Yeah, girl . . ."

"I'm so glad," I say. "Right now, I need something to look forward to for a change. My mama is really stressing me out."

"What happened?" Mimi asks.

I give them a quick rundown of her recent visit.

Rhyann shakes her head and says, "Wow . . . that's some crazy stuff right there. Now she's trying to move in with you and Miss Lucy."

"I don't know where she is, and I'm getting worried about her," I say. "I tried calling her cell phone, but it's been disconnected. She's not at the apartment anymore—she really was evicted."

Rhyann gives me a hug. "Your mama is a survivor, Kylie. I'm sure she's fine and you'll be hearing from her soon."

"You really think so?" I ask.

"She found you at the salon, and then here, didn't she? Your mom knows where you are, so she'll come to you when she's ready."

Chapter 19

Saturday is finally here and we're on our way to see Mary J. Blige. I can't believe I'm hanging with my girls in a stretch limo.

This is nice. Real nice.

When we arrive at the Coliseum, I cannot contain my excitement any longer.

"I've never had backstage passes to anywhere," I squeak in a high-pitched voice. "This is so cool. I'm like this close to the performers." Pacing back and forth, I say, "I can't believe it. Can y'all believe this. I'm here. Here backstage. *Coool.*"

Divine chuckles at my blabbering nonstop like an idiot. I don't think I've stopped talking since we stepped out of the limo—my first limo ride. I'm definitely not trying to go the princess route, but with my new dress, fresh perm, flat ironed hair, and VIP treatment, I feel like royalty.

"Kylie, if you're freaking out now, then I don't know what you're going to do when you meet my mom."

"Hey, I couldn't even go up into the pulpit at my grandma's church back home, so this is a really big deal for me," I say. "I can't believe I'm actually gonna meet Miss Mary J. and watch her sing from back here. Then we're spending the night at your house. *Wow.*"

I'm so happy right now that I break out into a little dance.

"Okaay," Divine utters. "Kylie, you just lost some cool points. Don't you ever do that dance again."

I laugh.

The concert is . . . I don't have any words for it. I have not had so much fun or danced so much in a long time.

Afterward, we are ushered back to our limo and head to Divine's house. I have never been there before. Her mother has been away for the past couple of weeks, so she and Alyssa have been staying with Mimi. Kara Matthews and her fiancé, Kevin Nash, are in town this weekend, and Divine's invited all of us to stay over.

I feel like I've stepped into heaven when I walk into the house. Mimi's house is large and beautifully decorated, but Divine's house seems twice as large.

My mouth drops open at the sight of her bedroom. "Divine, you can fit my whole town in here."

Her mother and Kevin are downstairs to greet us after we put our overnight bags in Divine's bedroom. They announce that we're having a late dinner, so we follow them into the dining room.

I've never seen a table that seats twelve people. *This is so nice,* I think to myself.

Divine looks over at me and says, "I think you should tell everyone the good news."

Everyone is watching me and waiting.

"I'm going back to school in the fall," I announce. "I have to take some online classes in addition to my regular schedule in order to graduate in time, but I'll do whatever it takes."

"That means you'll be graduating with us," Mimi realizes.

"I won't be at the same school with you," I say. "I'll be at Belmont High School and then community college. There's no way I can pay for Spelman, and I don't want to have to deal with student loans."

Divine's mother wipes her mouth with the edge of her napkin. She has an announcement of her own. "Kylie, I spoke to the headmaster at Stony Hills Prep and told him about you. He would like to set up a meeting with you and your mother. He's positive that he can get you a full scholarship, but even if he can't, I told him that I would pay your tuition. Marilee and I had a long conversation about you, and from what she's told me, I believe you would do well at Stony Hills Prep."

At this unbelievably great news, my eyes fill with tears and overflow. I wipe my face with my napkin. "You don't have to do that, Miss Kara."

"From everything Marilee has told me, I know that you have great potential. It truly takes a village to raise a child." She levels a finger at me. "I really believe that, and I'm willing to put my money where my mouth is, sweetheart."

"As for college, you don't have to worry about that, either," Kevin Nash contributes. "I would like to cover those expenses for you and Rhyann. I feel the same way as Kara." He motions around the grand dining room. "We have been blessed beyond measure, and we have the ability to provide you with a good education. Let us do that for you. You can pay us back by becoming the best you can be."

I wipe the tears from my eyes.

Rhyann says, "Thanks so much, Mr. Kevin, but I'm good. I already have an angel taking care of me. You take care of Kylie, and when we graduate from college and become established, we'll do the same for someone else."

"That's right," Kara agrees. "Pay it forward."

Finally, I find my voice. "Mr. Nash, I can't believe you want to do something like that for me. You, too, Miss Kara. Y'all don't even know me like that. I appreciate everything y'all doing for me, but I'm pretty sure I can get some scholarships, and I'm willing to work my way through school. My mama has taken too many handouts from people," I explain. "She doesn't think she needs to work for anything, and I don't want to be anything like her."

"I find that admirable," Kevin Nash replies. "However, I'm not offering you a handout. I'm investing in your future. I'm sowing into your life, and like Kara said—when you can, just pay it forward."

"Thank y'all so much," I manage through my tears. I send up a quick prayer to God for placing these people in my life. "I won't let you down. I promise."

We gather in Divine's room to give her mother and Kevin Nash some privacy.

"I can't believe I was invited to the wedding," I say when we change into our pajamas.

"Girl, we told you, Kylie. You're one of the fab five," Divine states. "You have to be there."

We stay up and talk most of the night. I'm having a wonderful time with my friends, but in the back of my mind, I can't forget about my mama. I'm worried that we haven't heard anything from her yet. Then again, she could be playing me.

I haven't forgotten how manipulative she can be. I just hate not knowing where she is and how she's living. I don't really want to care, but I do, because I love her. She's my mama.

Chapter 20

The sound of the doorbell cuts into my conversation with Miss Lucy. I was telling her about my date with Chandler and my visit to the USC campus.

"I'll get it, Miss Lucy," I shout, climbing off the leather sofa.

For a split second, I don't recognize the woman standing at the door. I haven't seen her in almost a month, and I've been so worried about her. *"Mama?"*

She nods and offers me a slight smile. "Yeah, it's me. Believe it or not, it's your mama."

I can't believe that woman wearing a short-sleeve, loose-fitting dress and no makeup is my mom. "I don't know what to say."

"You can let me into the apartment, for a start," she says soberly. "I'd like to talk to you, Kylie. No game or ulterior motive. I just want to talk."

Curious about this sudden change in her appearance and her demeanor, I step aside to let her enter.

She greets Miss Lucy and asks all the questions a concerned parent would ask while I stand there in shock.

My mama and Miss Lucy sit down on the sofa. Curious, I make myself comfortable on the floor.

"Mama, what's up with the outfit?" I ask.

"I've been thinking about everything you been telling me, and it's time that I make some changes in my life." She raises her eyes to meet my gaze. "Kylie, I love you, even though I might not show it all of the time, and the truth is that I don't wanna lose you. It hurt me something fierce when you ran away from home."

I don't respond.

"I got me a job," Mama blurts out. "It's just waitressing, but it's a job."

"That's great," I murmur. I feel like I am dreaming. For as long as I can remember, I've never known my mama to have any type of real job.

"Where are you staying?" I inquire, thinking she's probably gonna try and hit us up one more time. Mama surprises me, though. "I'm living with a friend for now, but I plan on getting a place real soon. A place for us."

Here we go. Some things just never change.

"So for how long this time?" I ask her, my voice tinged with frustration. "How long before we're running out in the middle of the night? I can't do that anymore. You don't know how long you'll be staying with this current man anyway."

"My friend is not a man," Mama quickly interjects. "I'm staying with a girlfriend. We're both trying to save money, so we are splitting the expenses on a one-bedroom. I sleep on the sofa bed. Kylie, I know you don't believe me, but I'ma change this time. I'm getting older and I don't have nothing to show for it."

I smile for the first time since she arrived. "I'm happy for you, Mama. I really am."

It's not a full smile because my mom has let me down so many times. She says this stuff and she will actually do right for a little while, but it never lasts. All I know is that my heart can't bear another disappointment. I'm trying to get myself together and I don't need my mom's troubles holding me back.

"Please give me another chance, Kylie," my mama pleads with me.

My arms folded across my chest, I respond, "I can't deal with the drama."

"I know I hurt you, Kylie, and I'm sorry." Her eyes grow wet with unshed tears. "I'm not perfect—nobody is—but I'm willing to try to better myself. I have missed you so much. Kylie, you were my best friend."

"That's part of the problem," I say. "I didn't want to be your friend. I wanted to be your daughter."

"I had you so young, I didn't know how to be a mom."

"I don't think anybody knows how to be a mother," I retort. "You have to just do it. Grandma Ellen raised me because you were never home. My problem is that you didn't even try to be a mom. You shouldn't have had me if you didn't want a child."

"I wanted you, Kylie," she countered. "Don't you ever think that I didn't. I loved you, but that did not stop me from wanting to have a life. I was young and I wanted to have fun."

"And you want me to believe that you don't want that anymore?"

"Not if it means losing you."

That stops me for a few moments. "Mama, I don't know what you want me to say. I'm glad you finally have a job and a place to live, but I'm pretty sure that in a few months, you'll be back to your old self."

My mom rises to her feet and shakes her head. "Kylie, not this time. I know that I let you down in the past, but I'm a different person now. You don't have to believe me, but I will show you."

I stand up as well, with my arms folded across my chest. "So where are you working?"

"The Red Lobster on Holt Street. It's not too far from here."

"You like it?"

She shrugs. "It's a job. I'm still looking for something better."

My mom sounds like she is sincere, but I'm still skeptical. This time I am going to just stand back and see what happens. I refuse to let her keep hurting me, and I can't depend on her.

She suddenly starts crying.

I glance over at Miss Lucy before embracing my mama. "Kylie, I messed up big-time—I know that. But that doesn't change the fact that I love you."

I don't like to see her cry. "Mama . . . don't . . . please stop crying."

She wipes away her tears with her fingertips. "I just don't want to lose you, Kylie. My life isn't the same with you gone."

"You say that now, but what about when the next man comes along? What then, Mama? I'm glad you're not a drug addict, but in a way it's not much different. You're addicted to men."

"No more," she vows. "Just you watch. I'm gonna show you, Kylie. I'ma prove it to you—I've changed, and you'll see." She marches to the door.

"Mama," I call out.

She stops.

"I love you, and congratulations on the job," I tell her.

She smiles through her tears. "I love you, too, baby."

When my mama leaves, Miss Lucy strolls out of the kitchen and takes a seat beside me. "She sure sounds like she means it, Kylie. When she was talking, all I saw on her face was repentance."

I'm not so easy to convince. "I think she just doesn't have a man right now."

"Don't be so hard on your mother."

"Miss Lucy, she probably wants to move in here with us," I say. "That's all that is, but we don't need her drama."

She is making a little shaking motion with her head. "I usually have a pretty good read on people. Serena is trying to change because of her love for you."

The girls come over an hour later.

"Kylie, why are you being so quiet?" Mimi asks me. "You okay?"

I nod.

Divine studies me a moment before saying, "No, you're not, Kylie. Now, what's up with you?"

Rhyann puts her hands on her hips. "Talk to us, girl."

"My mama came by the apartment today," I announce. "She told me that she has a job now."

Alyssa gives me a sidelong glance. "That's a good thing, right?"

"Only if she's serious about working," I say. "There's no point in working for a few weeks and then quitting. She claims that she's changed, and Miss Lucy believes her. I'm just not as sure."

"If Jerome can change, then I know your mom can change also," Divine tells me. "I didn't believe him at first, but he proved me wrong."

That gives me hope. "She told me that she was going to show me that she's telling the truth."

"Give her a chance," Divine says. "She's your mom. You two need each other."

"I don't need her."

"Kylie, don't say that," Rhyann interjects. "At least your mom is alive. I would give anything to have my mom walking around here, even if she wasn't acting like a mother."

I had not really considered how I'd feel if something terrible happened to my mama. I don't want to lose her.

"We know that you love your mom," Divine is saying. "You're just really mad at her right now. Kylie, don't hold on to all that anger. Forgive your mom and give her another chance. Think how you'd feel if you had done something bad. Wouldn't you want her to forgive you and give you a second chance?"

"Or a third?" Mimi asks.

"Or a fourth," Rhyann interjects.

"Even if you mess up a hundred times, you would still want a chance to get it right," Alyssa contributes. "Think about how many times we mess up with God, but we still want His forgiveness."

"You're right," I say at last. "I want to believe my mama about everything, even if she's let me down so many times in the past. I know what you're saying, Alyssa. It's not like I haven't made mistakes or bad choices. I don't want them held against me, and I'd want another chance." I chew on my bottom lip.

"Just take your relationship with your mother one day at a time, Kylie," Miss Lucy interjects. "That's really all you can do."

"I guess so," I say in a low voice.

My mama calls me every day just to check on me since she bought herself a prepaid cell phone. She even has a second job now.

She is a receptionist for some company on Wilshire Boulevard, and she works at Red Lobster on the weekends.

"I'm on my lunch break, but I wanted to tell you that I love you, Kylie. I also read all that stuff you gave me on that school. I think you should go there."

"I gave you that packet almost two months ago."

"I know. That was before I decided to change my life. It's not too late for you to attend, is it? I didn't mess it up for you, did I?"

"They are gonna want to meet with you. Mr. Nash is

paying my tuition, but they still need to meet you—and Miss Lucy, since I'm living here with her."

"Let me know when and I'll put in for a day off or at least half a day. Kylie, you won't believe it, but I have almost a thousand dollars saved. I have a bank account with the credit union."

My mouth drops open in my shock. "You have a bank account?"

She laughs. "Yeah, girl. It's only a savings account for right now. I would have more saved, but I have to pay off some stuff to raise my credit score. I'm taking a class on managing finances because I'd like to buy us a house one day. One of my coworkers was saying that I could qualify for one of those Habitat for Humanity houses. Maybe we could get us a three-bedroom house."

"Why three bedrooms?"

"We can't leave out Miss Lucy," she tells me. "She's family now."

Her words make me smile. "That would be nice. I'm really proud of you, Mama."

She sounds very pleased. "Well, I have to get back to work."

"Mama, why don't you come over on Sunday if you don't have to work? You could have dinner with us."

She jumps on that idea. "Honey, I'll come right after work," she says. "Thanks for inviting me to eat with y'all. You have no idea how much this means to me, Kylie."

I've been doing some thinking, and I've come to realize something very important. "None of us are perfect, and I have no right to judge you. You're my mama, and you deserve a second chance. I'm sorry for the way that I treated you."

"As Mama would say, truth is truth. You had every right to expect me to act like a mother. After all, I brought you into this world."

I'm not done, though. "Miss Lucy says that we shouldn't keep looking back into the past. She says that we should focus on the future. We're gonna start over, Mama."

"I'd really like that."

I smile. "I can't wait to see you."

"I'm proud of you," Miss Lucy tells me when I get off the phone.

"You were right," I admit. "If I want to be forgiven for the times I mess up, then I have to do the same. I realize that now. I also realize that my mama did the best that she could, I guess. By the time she was sixteen, I was two years old. She just wanted to be a teenager."

"I'm glad to see she's trying to be an adult now," Miss Lucy replies. "You need her to grow up so that she can be there to guide you."

"I know she's gonna make mistakes and all, but I'm gonna just love her."

"And keep the lines of communication open," Miss Lucy advises. "She needs you as much as you need her."

"She'll also have you to help keep her on the straight and narrow, as Grandma Ellen would say."

Miss Lucy laughs. "I'll keep you both straight."

She has been so good to me. "My grandma was right about something else. She used to always say that being related doesn't always make you a family—love is what makes you family. I lost her, but God brought you into my life."

She feels the same way. "I was never blessed to have any children, and I used to be sad about it, but like you said, God brought us together. We are a family."

I finally have the one thing I have wanted most in my life. I have my mama back and some wonderful friends and family. I don't have a lot of material possessions, but as far as I'm concerned, I am the richest girl in the world.

Readers Club Guide for

Split Ends

by Jacquelin Thomas

SYNOPSIS

Kylie Sanderson is sixteen and homeless, living on the streets of Los Angeles after running away from her neglectful mother, Serena. With no friends, no family, and no safe place to stay, she's scared and alone, until an older homeless woman and a kind local business owner take her under their wings, offering her a job at a well-known salon. Kylie becomes friends with her coworker Rhyann, and through her, she befriends Divine, Mimi, and Alyssa, forming the "fab five B.F.F. club." But Kylie has a secret she's keeping from everyone, and she knows that if they find out, it could ruin her newfound happiness. In the end, Kylie learns that true friends will stand by you no matter what, you can create your own family, and dreams sometimes do come true.

QUESTIONS FOR DISCUSSION

1. Do you think Kylie made the right decision to run away from her mother because their life together was too unstable, or did she jump into an even more chaotic and dangerous situation?

2. In her first couple of days on the streets, Kylie encounters other teenagers who have turned to drugs and shoplifting, and a pimp who tries to lure her into prostitution. Do you think if Kylie had not met Miss Lucy and Miss Marilee, she would have continued to resist, or would she have allowed herself to be pulled into that lifestyle in order to survive? What other options besides a life of crime are available to a teenager on the streets?

3. Before she meets Divine, Kylie reads about her in a magazine and fantasizes about how perfect her life must be. Why are we so inclined to think other people's lives, particularly those of celebrities, are so much better than our own? Is anyone ever completely happy, or is that a naïve assumption?

4. Miss Lucy is a former war veteran who turned to alcohol and ended up on the streets. Now she cannot receive her veteran's benefits because she has no address. Do you think it's common for people who have served their country to

fall between the cracks like this? Should there be better systems in place to ensure this doesn't happen?

5. Divine tells Kylie, "Stop being a victim. . . . we accept you as you are. The problem is that you seem to want us to change who we are. . . ." (page 196) While Kylie thinks that her friends are judging her, is she actually the one judging them? Can snobbery work in both directions?

6. Kylie is determined not to get too close to Chandler or any other boy, so that she's not distracted from her dreams of finishing high school and going to college. Do you think this is an unreasonable fear, based on her mother's relationships with men, or is this a valid concern? What did you think of Kylie's purity ring? Do you know anyone who has taken a purity vow?

7. When Mimi and Divine try to give Kylie some of their hand-me-down clothing, she doesn't want to accept it. Divine tells her, "God has blessed my family so that we can be a blessing to others." (page 148) Why is Kylie willing to accept help from Miss Marilee, but so reluctant to accept it from her friends? Do you agree with Divine that those who have been given many blessings have a responsibility to share those blessings?

8. Kylie tells Chandler, "The truth is that not all homeless people are druggies or have mental problems. They are

normal people like you and me. " (page 191) Did this make you think of homeless people differently? Did you have a preconceived notion of what homeless people are like, or what they had done to end up on the streets?

9. Kylie believes that if Serena really loved her, she would be a better mother, but Miss Marilee suggests that she might be doing the best she can, having given birth to Kylie when she was only fourteen. Do her circumstances excuse her behavior? Either way, does Kylie owe it to her mother to forgive her? Does Serena deserve respect, or must she, as Kylie says, earn that respect?

10. At the end of the novel, Kylie says, ". . . being related doesn't always make you family—love is what makes you a family." (page 231) What do you think about this statement? Is family based on bloodlines, or can it be a choice?

ACTIVITIES TO ENHANCE YOUR BOOK CLUB

1. On average, there are 1.35 million homeless children and 400,000 homeless veterans annually in the United States. To learn more about the problem, visit National Coalition of the Homeless at www.nationalhomeless.org.

2. Before they get their own apartment, Kylie and Miss Lucy rely heavily on the people at the Safe Harbor Mission. Get the members of your group together to volunteer at a local soup kitchen one Saturday, or help build a house with a Habitat for Humanity group.

3. Jacquelin Thomas has written a previous series of books about Divine and her friends. To learn more, visit www.SimplyDivineBooks.com.

A Conversation with Jacquelin Thomas

Q. You've written for both teenagers and adults. Does your process change from one to the other? Is there one audience you prefer writing for?

A. **I love writing for both audiences, and it's interesting that my audience as a whole seems to read both genres. I have adults who read the YA books and teens reading my adult books. The process is the same—only the mentality of my characters changes.**

Q. Kylie's friends are always pitching in to help each other. Do you have your own "B.F.F. club"? What are your best friends like?

A. **I don't have a lot of best friends, but the ones I have are wonderful! They know who I am and they still love me.**

Q. Mimi tells Kylie that "having each other's back is part of the B.F.F. code." What would you consider to be your basic rules of friendship? If you were writing a B.F.F. code, what would be in it?

A. **My rules would be:**
   1. **Be honest with each other.**

2. Know each other's faults and love each another in spite of them.
3. Have each other's back unless it's something illegal and/or immoral.
4. Show yourself worthy of their trust.

Q. You deal with some serious issues in *Split Ends,* such as panic disorder, homelessness, and abuse. What kind of research did you do in writing those scenes? How do you find the right balance between getting a message across and entertaining your readers?

A. I actually suffer from panic disorder, so I know from experience how anxiety can cripple you. I've volunteered to help the homeless and have heard their stories of how they ended up on the streets. I don't just set out to entertain my readers—I also want to educate them on real life, but not to the point of beating them over the head with my message. I want readers to pause for a moment and just consider what is going on, and how it relates to their experiences or of those of someone they may know.

Q. What made you decide to make the transition from writing traditional romance to writing with Christian themes?

A. It was my relationship with God. He has always been a

part of my life, and so it was natural to include Him in the world I created for my characters.

Q. Miss Marilee feels that she has been blessed so she can bless others, and puts a lot of emphasis on service, without expecting anything back. Is there someone who was there for you at a time when you really needed it?

A. Jesus said that He came to serve and not to be served. This is His desire for us as well. I've found true contentment whenever I'm helping others. I've had many angels in my lifetime—people who reached out to me when I needed them and I believe in paying it forward.

Q. Kylie and Miss Lucy use a lot of unusual expressions, like calling chicken the "gospel bird" (page 64) or saying a boy couldn't "hit a lick with a snake," (page 94) to mean that he wasn't ambitious. Are there any regional or family expressions you use that your readers may not have heard before?

A. I'm from Georgia, so the expressions in the book are the ones I grew up hearing.

Q. Who are your favorite writers? What do you read for fun?

A. I love mysteries and especially books by James Patterson, but I also love historical fiction, and read a lot of historical romance as well as most authors writing in the Christian fiction genre.

Q. Throughout the novel, the characters refer back to the Bible. Do you have a favorite passage from scripture? What is it, and why?

A. I guess it would be Habakkuk 3:17–19, because it talks about how Habakkuk lost everything, but he continued to rejoice in the Lord because God is his strength and has equipped him to endure trials and tribulations. I believe that we find out what we're really made of when we go through hardships. Oftentimes, we feel life isn't fair and we pout, but another way to look at our struggles is this: The harder the struggle, the more faith God has in us. He knows just how much we can bear, so when life gets rough, just know that God is there cheering you on, because He knows that you can make it through! He just wants you to realize it, too, and trust that He's already worked it out.

Q. Your previous novel, *Hidden Blessings*, was made into a movie. If *Split Ends* were a movie, are there actresses you picture for any of the roles?

A. Divine: KeKe Palmer (*True Jackson, VP; Akeelah and the Bee*)
Kylie: Erica Hubbard (*Lincoln Heights*)
Mimi: Sahara Garey (*Akeelah and the Bee; That's So Raven; Everybody Hates Chris*)
Rhyann: Kiely Williams (*The Cheetah Girls*)

Check out the Divine book that started it all!

simply *divine*

Available from Pocket Books

Mimi, I'm dying for you to see my dress," I say into the purple-rhinestone-studded cell phone. "It's this deep purple color with hand-painted scroll designs in gold on it. I have to be honest. I—Divine Matthews-Hardison—will be in *all* the magazines. I'll probably be listed in the top-ten best-dressed category."

Mimi laughs. "Me too. My dress is tight. It's silver and strapless and Lana Maxwell designed it."

"Oh, she's that new designer. Nobody really knows her yet." I'm hatin' on her because she's allowed to wear a strapless gown and I had to beg Mom for days to get her to let me wear a halter-style dress.

I make sure to keep my voice low so that the nosy man Mom claims is my dad can't hear my conversation. It's a wonder Jerome actually has a life of his own—he's always trying to meddle in mine.

I can tell our limo is nearing the entrance of the Los Angeles Convention Center because I hear people screaming, and see the rapid flashing of cameras as die-hard fans try to snap pictures of their favorite celebrities while others hold up signs. I'm glued to the window, checking out the growing sea of bystanders standing on both sides of the red carpet.

The annual Grammy Awards celebration is music's biggest night and the one major event I look forward to attending every year. Singers, actors and anyone really important will be present. Media coverage is heavy and I know as soon as I step out of the limo, the press is going to be all over me.

Settling back in the seat, I tell Mimi, "I'll talk to you when you get here. I need to make sure my hair is together. You know how these photographers are—they're like always trying to snap an ugly picture of celebrities to send all over the world. That's the last thing I need—some whack photo of me splashed all over the tabloids. See you in a minute. Bye."

Cameras flash and whirl as limo after stretch limo roll to a stop. I put away my phone and take out the small compact mirror I can't live without, making sure every strand of my hair is in place. A girl's gotta look her best, so I touch up my lips with Dior Addict Plastic Gloss in Euphoric Beige. I like this particular lip gloss because the color doesn't make my lips look shiny or too big in photographs.

I pull the folds of my gold-colored silk wrap together and blow a kiss to myself before slipping the mirror back into my matching gold clutch. I'm looking *fierce,* as my idol Tyra Banks loves to say on *America's Next Top Model.* To relieve some of the nervous energy I'm feeling, I begin tracing the pattern of my designer gown. This is my first time wearing what I consider a grown-up gown. I've never been able to wear backless before, but thankfully, my mom has a clue that I'm not a baby anymore. I'll be fifteen soon.

"Divine, honey, you look beautiful," Mom compliments. "Anya did a wonderful job designing this gown for you. It's absolutely perfect. Doesn't make you look too grown up."

My smile disappears. She just had to go there.

"Thanks." As an afterthought, I add, "You do too."

My mom, renowned singer and actress Kara Matthews, is up for several Grammys. On top of that, she's scored starring roles in three blockbuster movies, one of which will have her leaving in a couple of weeks to film the sequel in Canada. She can be pretty cool at times but then she goes and ruins it by going into Mom mode. To get even, I say and do things to wreck her nerves. Like . . .

"I hope I see Bow Wow tonight. He's so hot . . ." I can't even finish my sentence because the look on Mom's face throws me into giggles. My dad, Jerome, comes out of an alcohol-induced daze long enough to grumble something unintelligible.

He's never allowed me to call him daddy. Says it makes him feel old, so he insists that I call him Jerome.

Hellooo . . . get a clue. *You are old.*

It used to bother me that Jerome didn't want me calling him Dad when I was little. But after all the crazy stuff he's done, I'd rather not tell anyone he's related to me. Although I've never actually seen him drink or whatever, I've watched enough TV to know what an addict looks like. If I could sell him on eBay, I'd do it in a heartbeat. I can just picture the ad in my head.

Hollywood actor for sale. Okay-looking.
Used to be real popular until he started
drinking and doing drugs. By the way, he
really needs a family because he's on his
way out of this one. Bidding starts at one dollar.

Mom interrupts my plans to auction Jerome by saying, "Divine, I don't want you sniffing around those rap artists. You stay with me or Stella. *I mean it.* Don't go trying to sneak off like you usually do. I don't care if Dean Reuben lets Mimi run around loose. You better not!"

Mom and Jerome make a big deal for nothing over me talking to boys. Period. I'm fourteen and in the eighth grade. I'm not even allowed to date yet, so I don't know why they're always bugging whenever I mention meeting guys. I will admit I get a thrill out of the drama, so I figure giving them a scare every now and then can't hurt.

"You stay away from that Bow Wow," Jerome orders. "He's a nice kid, but you don't need to be up in his face. Don't let that fast tail Mimi get you in trouble."

This subject has so come and gone. All his drinking must be making him forgetful or something. Rolling my eyes heavenward, I pull out my cell phone, flip it open and call my best friend just to irritate him.

"Mimi, we're about to get out and stroll down the red carpet," I say loud enough for him to hear. "Where's your car now?" Mimi's dad is an actor too. He's always out of town working, which Mimi loves because then she can run all over her entertainment-lawyer mom. Her dad is the strict one in her family. For me, it's Mom. She's the only grown-up in my family.

Our limo stops moving. The driver gets out and walks around to the passenger door.

"We're here, Mimi. I'll see you in a few minutes." I hang up and slip the phone into my gold evening bag.

Cameras flashing, the media are practically climbing all over the limo. As usual, my mom starts complaining. But if the media isn't dogging her, her publicist comes up with something to get their attention, which isn't hard to do with my dad's constant legal battles. I just don't get Mom sometimes.

Mom claims she doesn't really like being in the spotlight and the center of attention, but me, I love it. I'm a Black American Princess and I'm not ashamed to admit it. I take pleasure in being pampered and waited on. Mostly, I love to shop and be able to purchase anything I want without ever looking at a price tag.

"I wish I had a cigarette," Mom blurts. "I'm so nervous."

I reach over, taking her hand in mine. "Don't worry about it. I hope you win, but even if you don't, it's still okay. At least you were nominated."

She smiles. "I know what you're saying, sweetie. And you're right, but I *do* want to win, Divine. I want this so badly."

"I know." Deep down, I want it just as bad as she does. I want Mom to win because then I'll have something to hold over that stupid Natalia Moon's head. Her mother is singer

Tyler Winters. As far as I'm concerned, the woman couldn't sing a note even if she bought and paid for it. And I'm pretty sure I'm not the only one who thinks so, because she's never been nominated for a Grammy.

The door to the limo opens.

Leo, our bodyguard, steps out first. He goes everywhere with us to protect us from our public. There are people out there who'll take it to the extreme to meet celebrities.

Mom's assistant, Stella, gets out of the car next. All around us, I hear people chanting, "Kara . . . Kara . . . Kara."

A few bystanders push forward, but are held back by thick, black velvet ropes and uniformed cops.

"They love you, Mom."

Smiling, my mom responds, "Yeah . . . they sure do, baby."

I'm so proud to have *the* Kara Matthews as my mom. She's thin and beautiful. Although she's only five feet five inches tall, she looks just like a model. I have her high cheekbones and smooth tawny complexion, but unfortunately, I'm also saddled with Jerome's full lips, bushy eyebrows and slanted eyes. Thankfully, I'm still cute.

"Hey, what about me? I got some fans out there. They didn't just come to see yo' mama. She wouldn't be where she is if it wasn't for me."

I glance over my shoulder at Jerome, but don't respond. He's such a loser.

I have a feeling that he's going to find a way to ruin this night for Mom. Then she'll get mad at him and they'll be arguing for the rest of the night.

I've overheard Mom talk about divorcing Jerome a few

times, but when he gets ready to leave, she begs him to stay. I wish they'd just break up because Jerome brings out the worst in Mom, according to Stella.

Stella turns and gestures for me to get out of the limo. It's time to meet my public.

Okay . . . my mom's fans. But in a way, I'm famous too. I'm Hollywood royalty. Kara Matthews's beloved daughter.

I exit the limo with Leo's assistance. Jerome will follow me, getting out before Mom. She is always last. Her way of making an entrance, I suppose.

I spot a camera aimed in my direction. I smile and toss my dark, shoulder-length hair across my shoulders the very same way I've seen Mom do millions of times.

Mom makes her grand appearance on the red carpet amid cheers, hand clapping and whistles. We pose for pictures.

Here we are, pretending to be this close and loving family. What a joke!

I keep my practiced smile in place despite the blinding, flashing darts of lights stabbing at my eyes. It's my duty to play up to the cameras, the fans and the media.

I can't imagine my life any other way.

After a few poses in front of the limo, we start down the red carpet. Whenever I can, I stand in front of my parents, grinning like the Cheshire Cat in *Alice's Adventures in Wonderland*. I love being photographed and I know how to strike a perfect pose.

America's next top model—right here. As soon as I turn eighteen, I'm auditioning for that show. Mom says I won't have to. She actually had the nerve to tell me that I could be working right now as a model. Only she won't let me because she's real big on education, so I have to finish school first. Talk about dangling a pot of gold in front of my face and snatching it away.

Stella and Leo march in front of us, leading the way to the doors of the convention center.

I'm walking in front of my parents, close enough to hear Mom's words to Jerome.

"Do you have to manhandle me? You nearly ripped off my arm back there when you grabbed me."

I notice that Mom is careful not to move her lips for fear some reporter might be able to read her words. She's always trying to keep up appearances.

"Just 'cause you up for some awards, don't start acting like you don't know me," Jerome warns. "I'm the man of the house. I run thangs . . ."

"You don't run nothing," Mom shoots back. "When is the last time anyone called you for a job?"

"Could you please stop arguing?" The words just rush out of my mouth. "You're embarrassing me."

We run into another group of photographers.

Mom stops and leans against Jerome, wrapping her arms around him and wearing what everyone in the industry calls her million-dollar smile.

Well, I'm not about to be outdone.

I insert myself between my parents, separating them while tilting my face just right so that my best side will be photographed—just the way Mom taught me.

Jerome places his cold lips to my cheek, trying to show

off for the media. After a few more photos he breezes past us and into the convention center.

"I hate him," I mutter under my breath.

"Don't say that, Divine. He's your daddy."

Mom pauses to be interviewed, so I reach into my purse and pull out my cell phone. Pressing the talk button, I place it to my ear. "Mimi, where are you?"

I give Mom a big hug in the press room after the awards. "I'm sorry you only won the Grammy for Contemporary R&B Album."

Smiling down at me, Mom holds the coveted award close to her breast. "Sugar, I'm just thankful for this one. That album didn't do as well as my others, so I'm amazed *Living for You* actually won. This validates me personally."

Looking high as a kite, Jerome clumsily drapes his arm around her. "Okay, baby girl . . . it's time for you to go home. Mama and Daddy wanna party."

Pouting, I look up at Mom. "Do I really have to leave right now? I wanted to hang out for a little while longer."

"Well, you ain't doin' nothing but going home," Jerome rudely interjects. Like I was talking to him in the first place. "I don't want you hanging round these li'l dudes. You too young. I don' wanna hafta kill nobody 'bout my shorty."

Mom tries the diplomatic approach. "I know how much you want to stay, but your daddy's right, hon. Besides, you have to go to school tomorrow and you're not exactly a morning person. We girls need our beauty rest."

"Mom, I know you can come up with something better than that. I'm cute—losing one night of sleep won't hurt me. Why can't I just pop into one party at least? I don't have to stay long. Just enough to say I went. All the other kids at school will be talking about the parties they went to." I impatiently push away a stray curl from my face. "I'm not a baby. I'm almost fifteen."

Jerome bristles. "We know how old you are, Divine. We were there when you were born. Remember?"

I'm not ready to give up, so I keep pushing. "Then why can't I go for a little while? Mimi's dad is real strict but he's letting her go to the party with them at the House of Blues. Tomorrow's Valentine's Day. This can be one of my presents."

Mom places a gentle hand to my cheek. "Hon, we're not changing our minds. You're going home and that's final."

I release a long sigh in my frustration. My parents never let me have any fun. They're ruining my life.

Mom hugs me. This is her attempt to soothe me but the effort is totally wasted because I'm really mad at her.

"How about we go shopping tomorrow after school? We'll go to the Beverly Center and Rodeo Drive."

At the mention of shopping, my spirits lift some. If Mom insists on switching to Mom mode, then I plan to punish her by spending as much of her money as I can. This time it's really going to cost her big. "I want to go to Gucci and Louis Vuitton because I need to get a couple of new purses. Then I want to see the new collection at Iceberg."

"We can do that too," Mom promises. "Whatever you want."

"I don't have to go shopping with Stella, do I?" The last time we were to go shopping, Mom backed out to do a radio interview to promote her album.

"No, you don't," Mom assures me. "Tomorrow, you and I are going to spend some much-needed quality time together. I promise." She glances over her shoulder at Jerome. "Daddy's gonna join us if he's not too busy. Right?"

Jerome sends Mom a strange look I can't decipher.

I really don't want Jerome tagging along. All he ever does is complain about standing around while we try on clothes, or he fusses about how much money we spend. It isn't like we're spending any of his money. Mom is the one making paper.

"I might be able to make it but don't hold me to it."

I hope that Jerome's not able to join us. He's such a loser.

Stella comes over to where we're standing. "C'mon, Divine. It's time I got you home."

I glance over at Mom, giving her one last chance to change her mind. "I don't want to leave just yet. Nelly is right over there. Can I just go over there to meet him before I leave?"

"For what?" Jerome demands. "You better just take yo' lil fast tail home."

"You need to shut up. It's not even like that. I just want to meet him so that I can tell everyone that I met him." I don't include that my friend Rhyann and I have a fifty-dollar bet to see who'll meet him first.

He leans over and plants a kiss on my forehead. "You my baby girl. I'm just tryin' not to let you grow up too fast. You know I love you."

I push him away, no longer caring who's watching us. I don't need Jerome trying to act like a father now. "Leave me alone, Jerome. You are so not related to me."

"Sugar, don't do that," Mom whispers. "Remember, we've talked about this. Be nice to your daddy. There's a photographer in the corner watching us." Smiling, she adds, "Now give me a hug."

Embracing Mom, I feign a smile. This is really going to cost her big.

"I love you," she whispers.

Whatever. Right now, Mom's entering the loser zone in a big way.

Jerome purses his lips as if waiting for me to kiss him, but he'll turn blue and green before that ever happens. I walk off toward the nearest exit with Stella following. She makes a quick call to have our driver bring the limo around.

Without a word spoken between us, I climb into the limo, turn on the small television and settle back for the forty-five-minute drive home to Pacific Palisades.

Mom's face appears on the small screen.

"Could you turn that up, please?"

Stella turns up the volume.

It's a clip of Mom's interview after her Grammy win. I smile. "She looks real happy, doesn't she?"

"Yes, she does," Stella murmurs. "I believe her whole world is going to change after tonight."

I like seeing my mom happy. Lately though, I've noticed that she spends a lot of time in her bedroom with the door locked. The few times I've put my face to the door I've smelled the putrid odor of marijuana. I know Jerome has been smoking the stuff for years. But for Mom I think this is something new.

I've never told anyone because Stella and Mom are always saying, "What's done at home stays at home. You never betray family."

It really bothers me that my parents smoke marijuana, especially Mom. Just last year, she was the keynote speaker at my school's drug-awareness program.

What a hypocrite.

It's all Jerome's fault.

His constant legal battles and a recent paternity suit have taken a toll on my mom. At least that's what I overheard Mom telling Stella a few days ago.

"Do you think Mom will divorce Jerome?"

Stella put away her cell phone. "Divine, you don't need to worry yourself with grown-up matters."

"Well, I hope she does," I confess. "Mom would be much happier if she did."

"Let's not talk about this right now," Stella whispers. "Divine, you really need to be very careful about what you say in public."

A small sigh escapes me. The last thing I need right now is another lecture, especially one from a nonparent. Just because she and Mom grew up together, Stella thinks she can boss me around, but she's nothing more than the help as far as I'm concerned. She better be glad I halfway like her because otherwise she would've been fired a long time ago.

Want more teen fiction fun?
Check out these titles:

FAIR-WEATHER FRIENDS
ReShonda Tate Billingsley

GETTING EVEN
ReShonda Tate Billingsley

WITH FRIENDS LIKE THESE
ReShonda Tate Billingsley

BLESSINGS IN DISGUISE
ReShonda Tate Billingsley

NOTHING BUT DRAMA
ReShonda Tate Billingsley

Trouble In My Way
Michelle Stimpson

THE EXORSISTAH

It's a CURL THING
JACQUELIN THOMAS

Split ENDS
JACQUELIN THOMAS

X RETURNS
THE EXORSISTAH 2